# THE MAN OF HER DREAMS

"Sir Simon!"

"Ach, so you know my name?" he asked. It was odd
that he couldn't place her. He was usually quite good
with faces. She was very young, of course. Her dark
wool habit was that of a schoolgirl.

"Yes, I happened to overhear it . . . in the Pump
Room, I believe," said Sincerity, relieved that he didn't
recognize her.

"Then you have the better of me, Miss . . . ?"

"Hartford, sir. And I am sorry to be in your way," she
said, her smile putting the sun to shame—or so Simon
thought.

"Not at all. It was getting a bit late to be drawing
anyway," he replied with a smile. He reached up to pluck
her off her horse. Perhaps she was not so very young
after all, he decided, looking up at her engaging face as
his hands encircled her waist. It was the childish habit
and the braids that had fooled him. But with those
curves, she was certainly not a child.

Suddenly, alarms sounded in his head, and he would
have released Miss Hartford if it wouldn't have caused
her to fall on her face. What if she hadn't just happened
along? What if this young woman knew about his forays
to the cliffs to draw and was trying to entrap him?
Frowning mightily, he quickly completed his task, dropping his hands immediately.

Sincerity, being lifted gently to the ground, didn't notice his change of mood, and she smiled at him again,
her blue eyes wide and innocent. His nostrils breathed
in the hint of lavender from her hair.

"Thank you," she said softly.

"Oh, think nothing of it," he said blithely, promising
himself he would not encourage her. But his resolution
exploded like a flash of lightning when he looked into
those eyes. . . .

# BOOK YOUR PLACE ON OUR WEBSITE AND MAKE THE READING CONNECTION!

We've created a customized website just for our very special readers, where you can get the inside scoop on everything that's going on with Zebra, Pinnacle and Kensington books.

When you come online, you'll have the exciting opportunity to:

- View covers of upcoming books
- Read sample chapters
- Learn about our future publishing schedule (listed by publication month *and author*)
- Find out when your favorite authors will be visiting a city near you
- Search for and order backlist books from our online catalog
- Check out author bios and background information
- Send e-mail to your favorite authors
- Meet the Kensington staff online
- Join us in weekly chats with authors, readers and other guests
- Get writing guidelines
- AND MUCH MORE!

**Visit our website at http://www.zebrabooks.com**

# A TANGLED WEB

## DONNA BELL

# ZEBRA BOOKS
## Kensington Publishing Corp.
http://www.zebrabooks.com

ZEBRA BOOKS are published by

Kensington Publishing Corp.
850 Third Avenue
New York, NY 10022

Copyright © 2001 by Donna Bell

All rights reserved. No part of this book may be reproduced in
any form or by any means without the prior written consent of
the Publisher, excepting brief quotes used in reviews.

If you purchased this book without a cover you should be aware
that this book is stolen property. It was reported as "unsold and
destroyed" to the Publisher and neither the Author nor the Publisher has received any payment for this "stripped book."

All Kensington titles, imprints, and distributed lines are avail-
able at special quantity discounts for bulk purchases for sales
promotion, premiums, fund-raising, educational or institutional
use.

Special book excerpts or customized printings can also be created to fit specific needs. For details, write or phone the office
of the Kensington Special Sales Manager: Kensington Publishing Corp., 850 Third Avenue, New York, NY 10022. Attn. Special Sales Department. Phone: 1-800-221-2647.

Zebra and the Z logo Reg. U.S. Pat. & TM Off.

First Printing: July 2001
10 9 8 7 6 5 4 3 2 1

Printed in the United States of America

*With thanks to my editor*
*Tracy Bernstein*
*who enabled me to give life to*
*Sincerity, the third Hartford sister*

# ONE

"Miss Hartford, surely you know the depth of my feelings for you. I fear I am not capable of flowery words and poetry, but you cannot be unaware of my sentiments. I have spoken to your father, and he has granted me permission to speak to you."

As the large man leaned forward, his corsets creaked, rending the silence of the paneled study. Sincerity covered her smile with her hand.

"Sir, you do me a great honor, but you have taken me by surprise. I assure you, I never aspired to such an honor."

"But, Miss Hartford . . . Sincerity, surely my constant attentions haven't gone unnoticed," said the large, soberly garbed gentleman, covering her delicate fingers with his gloved hand.

Sincerity Hartford lowered her head, hiding her face from him. He dropped to one knee, his corsets protesting loudly, and looked up at her, his plain face entreating her to respond.

She hesitated. How could she not? She was not without sympathy. It was just that she held no tender feelings for Lord Hawkfield. Shaking her head slightly, she pulled back her hands, once again folding them neatly in her lap.

"I am sorry, my lord, if I have given you the wrong impression, but I fear we would not suit."

He rose, his face turning thunderous. "And I am sorry to have importuned you, Miss Hartford. Good day."

He strode to the door and Sincerity breathed a sigh of relief, but it was premature, for he stopped and turned back, favoring her with a cold glare.

"I don't wish to be rude, Miss Hartford, but I must ask you one question. Why, exactly, did you come to London this Season?"

Her own temper rising, she raised one brow and with a practiced toss of her golden curls responded, "Why does any young lady come to London, my lord?"

"Presumably to find a husband! But you . . . People have begun placing wagers on your accepting a suitor, any suitor, you know. I thought it mad, but after this interview . . ."

"They are placing wagers on me at the clubs?" she breathed, turning pale.

"Is it any wonder, Miss Hartford? Just how many Seasons have you spent in London? Three? Four?"

"Good day, my lord," said Sincerity, bowing her head once again. Her slender shoulders trembled with some undefined emotion, but she refused to be drawn. He gave an angry grunt and stalked away.

When the door closed, she looked up, a nervous giggle escaping her lips. "Lord Hawkfield is not as thick as I thought," she murmured.

The door to the study flew open, slamming against the wall with a force that shook the room.

"What the deuce are you about, hoyden?" growled her father, his shoulders filling the threshold and blocking the entrance of her petite mother who was sobbing loudly.

Sincerity leaped to her feet. "Papa!"

"Don't you 'Papa' me, young lady! Why the devil did

you turn down Hawkfield? What could you possibly have found to object to about the man?"

"Why, nothing, Papa, but I don't love him."

"Love him?" screeched her mother, passing her husband and coming swiftly toward her daughter, her hand upraised.

Lord Hartford caught her hand and held it. "Surely there is no need for that, Divinity. Let us at least hear her out." He guided his trembling wife to a chair before joining Sincerity on the sofa.

"What did he do, child, to give you a disgust of him?"

Under her father's kind gaze, Sincerity found it difficult to prevaricate. But she also knew her father would stand by her side against her mother's wrath for only so long before he washed his hands of the matter.

"He frightened me, Papa. He's just so tall, so large," she lied.

Her mother gave a snort of disbelief.

"He's the same height as I am, my dear girl, and I don't think you are frightened of *me*, now, are you?"

"Of course not, Papa, but you are trim and elegant. Lord Hawkfield, however, is so very massive. I find him overpowering. I cannot imagine . . . That is, I am so very small; it is difficult to picture myself as his wife."

The image her words evoked gave her father pause, and he patted her hand. "Well, we do not want to frighten you, puss," said her father, chucking her under the chin, "but we do want to see you settled. For all his size, I think Hawkfield would have made you an excellent husband. But I understand that he might have taken you by surprise."

"Thank you, Papa," she said quietly.

"However, Sincerity, your mother and I have only so much patience. You are three-and-twenty years, my dear, well past the age to wed. Your mother and I only want you to be happy, and what greater happiness is there for a woman than to have a husband and children? Therefore, might I suggest you look about you with that object in mind?"

"Yes, Papa," she replied, her eyes shining with unshed tears at his forbearance. "I will try."

He rose and added, "And one more thing, child. Do try to discourage the gentlemen that you don't find suitable. It is most unbecoming of a lady to encourage a gentleman whom she has no liking for."

"I'll try, Papa."

"I know you will. You're a good daughter, and though I'll be sorry to see you go, I want you to be happy. So remember what I've said." At the door, he looked back at his wife and daughter, so alike in appearance, so different in personality. "Divinity, are you coming?"

"In a few minutes, Herbert."

"Very well, but do not scold the girl. She can't help it if she is too kind to head off this sort of thing, or if the man is too much of a sapskull to understand." With that Lord Hartford closed the door, leaving his youngest daughter to face the wolf alone.

"This is the last time, Sincerity, that you will turn down a suitable match. You will marry, my girl, for I refuse to continue to foot the bill, Season after Season, with no results. People are beginning to wonder what is the matter with you, Sincerity. Here you are, three-and-twenty, and still unwed."

"I'm sorry to be such a disappointment to you, Mother," said the petite young woman, bowing her head so that the sun shining through the window would light her mop of blond curls like a halo. The effect, however, failed to move her steely eyed mother.

"When I think of how many opportunities, the countless offers, you have had over the past five years, young lady, I can't help but be disappointed. Here you are, every bit as pretty as your twin sister, Tranquility, but you have made almost no effort to secure a husband."

"Perhaps I have simply not met the right man," offered Sincerity in a small, unintrusive voice.

"The right man! Where do you come by these bourgeois notions, child? The right man just left!"

"But Lord Hawkfield—"

"Is everything a girl could want in a husband. He has both money and land, and as an added attraction, he is kind!"

"But I don't love him, Mama!"

"Love, bah! What on earth makes you think your purpose in wedding is to find love?" said Lady Hartford, rising and striding around the room once before returning and pointing her beringed finger at her youngest daughter. "I blame your sisters for putting such nonsensical notions into your head!"

"Love is not nonsense, Mother!"

Blue eyes met and held for one stormy moment before Lady Hartford sat down on the sofa. She looked away and said quietly, "Perhaps your sisters were lucky, Sincerity. I really can't say for sure. Perhaps, if you were to ask them now, they would tell you their lives are wonderful, that their love for their husbands hasn't diminished. I can only say what I know of the world. A marriage based on mutual respect is the best sort of marriage. Respect doesn't fade with time."

"But, Mama, I want more than respect," said Sincerity, reaching out and touching her mother's hand. Her mother flinched, but she didn't withdraw her hand.

"You know I didn't approve of either of your sisters' choices. Oh, Chastity did well enough in selecting Fitzsimmons since she will have enough money for them both one day, but they went about it in such a havey-cavey manner."

"But you adore little Andrew and Hope," said Sincerity.

"Of course I do. But Tranquility . . ."

"She is happy, Mother," said Tranquility's twin firmly.

"Perhaps, though I don't see how anyone can be happy and penniless at the same time. And you haven't seen that ramshackle chateau they inhabit!" said Lady Hartford, her voice rising as she hit upon a favorite complaint.

Sincerity rolled her eyes and sighed. "According to the letters she writes to me, she is exceedingly happy, especially now that she and Dominick are to have a baby!"

Lady Hartford shuddered. "What a relief that was that she was not already *enceinte* when they wed two years ago. I was so afraid . . ." She allowed this thought to remain unspoken as her daughter stared at her thoughtfully. Taking Sincerity's hands in hers, she put on a brave face and a brittle smile. "You must understand, my dear, you are my last hope. Both of your sisters were wed with such haste, that it was bound to cause a scandal. I want you to find someone, announce the betrothal, plan the wedding and trousseau, and finally, after several months of balls and galas to celebrate the coming event, wed your future husband with all the pomp and ceremony befitting such an occasion for someone of our station. Surely you would not deny me that?"

"I'll try, Mother. I really will try," said Sincerity, opening her blue eyes to their widest and meeting her mother's gaze without blinking. Lady Hartford patted her daughter's hand and rose, smoothing her skirts before bestowing one last smile and floating regally from the room.

"I'll try," Sincerity muttered, "but it's not going to work." With a sigh, she pried the novel she had been reading from between the cushions where she had stashed it upon Lord Hawkfield's arrival.

Opening it, Sincerity read a few pages, a frown creasing her brow. Really, the heroine's adventures were so much more enjoyable than her boring life. And she didn't have a perfect mother always breathing down her neck to "find a husband and settle down." Lucky heroine. All she had to worry about was how she was going to escape from the villain's castle!

"I worry so about him, Robbie. Angus told me he doesn't sleep for days on end," said the young lady, her voice soft and lilting.

"Surely you exaggerate, my dear. He looks much too fit to have missed so much sleep," replied the young man by her side, his gaze flitting toward the subject of their conversation only briefly before returning to her shell-like ear.

"A little perhaps, but you must see how very restless he is. His face is drawn, and there are dark circles under his eyes. And I swear he has lost weight. I hate to see him so."

"Shall I speak to him again?" whispered the young man.

"I wish the devil someone would speak to me," thundered the brawny man standing beside the fireplace, brandy swirling in the glass he was holding. He tossed off the contents and placed the glass on the mantelpiece before striding across the room and sitting down in the chair across from his sister and her earnest fiancé.

"Simon, there is no need to shout," said the young man, frowning fiercely.

"Isn't there? You act as if I were a child or some sort of beast, unable to understand what you're saying about me. So I am forced to speak up, hoping you will speak to me instead of whispering behind my back."

"Well, there's certainly nothing wrong with your hearing," laughed the young man.

"I'm sorry, Simon, but I am so worried about you."

"There is no need, my dear. I am fine. Perhaps I have been a bit restless since returning to Scotland, but I will settle down. It will take time."

"But, Simon, I can't feel right about leaving you when you are so unhappy."

"Really, Jessie, you aren't thinking of postponing our wedding!" exclaimed the young man.

Simon McKendrick gave a shout of laughter and said, "I thought that would have you pronouncing me fit as a fiddle, my good physician friend. Your concern for me flies out the window when it might mean waiting to take my sister down the aisle."

"Well, I do have my priorities," said the young physician with a self-deprecating chuckle. "But as I have told your loving sister, the problem is not physical so much as it is emotional. What you really need is a change of scenery. The Season is in full swing in London, you know."

"What, leave home again? No, after eight years of fighting, I'm back where I belong, and I'm not going anywhere, especially not to London. I made the mistake of going there for the Season once; nothing but grasping mamas and their equally heartless daughters."

"Simon, please. Robbie is only trying to help. And I am so very worried about you. I don't see how I can go off and leave you now."

Simon McKendrick looked down at his young sister and his frown faded. How could it not? She was the image of their late mother. Everything he believed about home and family was now wrapped up in this young woman and her future. If his Annie had lived, or even the babe—but that was in the past, he reminded himself firmly. For him, there was no future.

He forced a smile to his lips and turned to Robert Selkirk. "You see how she will lead you around by the nose, Robbie. Are you sure it's marrying the chit that you want?"

"More than life itself," said the young man, his eyes straying to his fiancée.

"Then first we will have a wedding. . . ."

"But, Simon . . ."

He held up his hand to silence his sister. "And then I will take a little trip. I have friends who are spending the spring in Bath. Perhaps I will go there, like an old man. I might even drink the waters."

"Oh, thank you, Simon. But you must also attend the assemblies and go to the Pump Room. I know it is not as fashionable as London, but you must make yourself go about in society."

"You see, Robbie?"

"She's only prescribing what I would. Only if I were you, my friend, I wouldn't touch that water. A more nasty concoction you'll never taste. My teacher advised me to try it once before recommending it to my patients. Since then, I've never told anyone to 'drink the waters.' "

"What, not in your whole, long career?" teased his future brother-in-law, smiling fondly at the young man who would wed his beloved sister.

"Very well. Poke fun at me if you wish. But if you try the waters, you have only yourself to blame."

"It is not the waters you need, Simon, it is the company," said his sister.

"So that is your prescription, my wise, old sister?" teased Simon.

She colored up prettily even as she nodded vigorously.

Sir Simon McKendrick grew serious and said, "Jessie, just don't get your hopes up and don't expect me to come home with a wife. I'm only agreeing in order to appease you and Robbie, so you'll go ahead and wed as planned.

I daresay it will do me good to get away from the keep, but a month or two in Bath is hardly enough to create a miracle," he finished, rising and patting his sister on the top of the head before strolling out the door of the salon, leaving her alone with her soon-to-be husband.

"We succeeded, my love. Now you may rest easy," said Robbie.

"I only hope it will do some good. Simon may not be expecting a miracle, but I will be praying for one," she said quietly.


"Miss Hartford, will you do me the honor of becoming my wife?" asked the young man kneeling in front of her.

He wore a spotted belcher neckcloth and had a large daisy protruding from the top buttonhole of his fitted coat. Sincerity barely refrained from giggling at the absurd picture he presented. The coat was a hideous pea green while his pantaloons were a dark purple. He looked like one of the circus performers at Astley's. A small giggle escaped her lips, but she rapidly turned it into a hacking cough. He scrambled to his feet and began pounding her back until she waved him away.

"There, there, Miss Hartford. Are you quite all right now?"

Really, he was a sweet boy. She judged him to be about her own age, but newly come to town and almost as green as his coat.

The thought of that coat brought on a fresh giggle that she covered with another cough. When he had finished whacking her back, he again asked anxiously after her health.

Clearing her throat weakly, Sincerity favored him with a wan smile. "I must confess, Lord Phipps, that I have not been very well lately. The physician . . . But I shouldn't burden you with my problems. It wouldn't be . . ." She gave a strangled cough before smiling up at him again.

He took a step back, then forward, indecision written clearly on his youthful brow.

"I had no idea, Miss Hartford. I . . ."

"Of course you did not. And really, you mustn't tell anyone."

"Your mother . . ."

"Especially my mother!" said Sincerity, her color fleeing from her face quite naturally at the thought. "That is, it upsets her so to discuss it. You understand."

"Of course," he said, looking toward the door and freedom.

"You don't know how happy it makes me to know that I have managed to capture your affections, Lord Phipps, but truly, you understand, that I cannot possibly accept at this time." She gave a delicate cough into her lace handkerchief before smiling up at him again.

"I understand. I'm sorry, uh, devastated, of course, but you must concentrate on getting better."

"Yes . . . I . . . will," she whispered, applying the scrap of lace to the corner of her eye. Lord Phipps took her hand, lifting it to his lips before he dropped it with a nervous twitch, bowed, and fled.

After a few minutes, Sincerity once again wiped her eyes, this time to dry the tears her laughter had produced. The clock began to strike the hour, and she rose, hurrying to her room to change into a carriage dress.

Tying the blue ribbon on her bonnet just under her ear, Sincerity jumped when the door to her chamber opened. When she saw her former governess, she relaxed.

"It's just me," whispered Miss Cobb.

"Come inside and shut the door, Cobbie. I'm going out to, uh, find some new lace to trim that green gown."

"You needn't make up tarradiddles for me, Sincerity.

*Donna Bell*

I know very well why you are so anxious to be out of the house."

"Then help me button up the back of this gown, and then go and fetch your bonnet. I would much rather have your company than Marnie's."

"That is because Marnie reports to your mother," said the observant Miss Cobb. "But, Sincerity, you are only postponing the inevitable, my dear. Your mother will be livid when she discovers Lord Phipps made an offer and you turned him down just like all the others."

"Since Lord Phipps didn't bother to speak to my father first, perhaps Mother will not find out," said Sincerity with a sly smile.

"And perhaps the sun will not rise tomorrow. Really, Sincerity, one would think you didn't want to marry," said the governess-turned-companion.

"And why would I? All I shall be doing is changing one form of slavery for another," she said dramatically.

"Hardly slavery," said Cobbie, glancing pointedly around the luxurious bedroom with its soft bed and warm fireplace.

"You know what I mean," came the petulant reply. "I have spent my entire life doing my mother's bidding. A husband would prove no different, perhaps even worse."

"My goodness, Sissie, if I didn't know better, I would suspect you of being bluestocking, or worse, a follower of that scribbler who wrote something about the rights of women."

"Mary Wollstonecraft? No, you know me better than that, although I do agree with many of the things she has written. What I do not want is a husband who tells me what to do, who to see, and where to live."

"But what of children?" asked the companion wistfully.

"After caring for me and my sisters all these years, Cobbie, I am surprised that you, of all people, would wax sentimental over the idea of having a bunch of troublesome brats."

"One of these days, Sincerity, you'll change your tune. One of these days . . ."

"In the meanwhile, Cobbie, let us make haste to be gone before Mother returns from her calls. The longer I can avoid her scold, the better."

"It is late, Sincerity. If we don't return home soon, your mother will call out the Bow Street Runners."

"I know, I know. I can't put it off any longer. And perhaps she will not have found out about Lord Phipps's proposal," said the pretty blonde, peering up at her companion hopefully.

Miss Cobb only shook her head and pointed to the carriage.

"Why did you turn down Lord Phipps?" asked the former governess after they had settled into the carriage, their packages stacked on the opposite seat.

"You know why. He is the most vapid goose I have ever had the misfortune to meet. Oh, I'll grant you he is well enough to look at, but that dreadful poetry he spouts, trying to sound bookish . . . Please! It is enough to give me a strong case of the vapors."

"But he is kind enough and certainly has enough money."

Sincerity turned to stare at her companion in the fading light, her blue eyes as round as her mouth, as she breathed an annoyed, "Oh, how can you say such a thing, Cobbie? I thought I could count on you to understand!"

"I do, my dear child. I do. But I know that your mother is not going to let this Season pass without seeing you betrothed and wed. You had better quit wasting time and decide which of your suitors you can tolerate the best."

"I know. I know," said Sincerity glumly. "If only I

could meet someone like Alex or Dominick. My sisters were so lucky."

Cobbie patted her charge's hand as they rounded the corner onto the quiet, fashionable street where the Hartford town house was situated.

"Tell me, Sissie, what did you do to discourage the man this time?" whispered the companion.

Sincerity's eyes sparkled as she related the story of her supposed illness that had kept her latest suitor at bay.

"Inspired!" Miss Cobb was continually amazed at her charge's fertile imagination.

"I thought so," whispered Sincerity with a nervous giggle as they entered the hall.

Then she spied her mother standing by the door to the salon, her expression stormy. Her father stepped out of his study, looked from his wife to his youngest daughter, and shook his head before withdrawing and closing the door.

"In here, Sincerity," said Lady Hartford. "Alone," she added when the companion started forward as well.

"Good luck," whispered Miss Cobb, squeezing Sincerity's hand.

"Exiled like a veritable criminal!" wailed Sincerity, staring out the window at the park that surrounded Hartford Manor. Spring flowers were just pushing out of the ground, but she found this only added to her dissatisfaction at being returned to her country home on the southern coast of England.

"At least you have the run of the estate, my dear. Your mother would have had the right to restrict you to your room on a diet of bread and water after all the whiskers you have told."

"Cobbie, I am three and twenty, hardly an age to be sent to my room."

"True," said her gray-haired companion. "If it weren't for your father, I daresay your mother would have disowned you. Really, Sincerity, letting Lord Phipps think you had consumption!"

"Well, it was better than marrying the man," grumbled Sincerity, her blue eyes beginning to twinkle. "And it was almost worth it to see the look of horror in his eyes when he reached for my hand to kiss it, then realized he might be infecting himself. I do believe he was about to cry."

"Wicked girl!" said Cobbie, her words softened by a smile.

"Yes, but I think this is punishment enough: sent home with my mother for the remainder of the Season so that I can be 'cured.' But never fear, I have taken steps."

"What steps?" asked Miss Cobb warily.

"I have written to Tranquility and to Chastity and begged for an invitation. Who better to understand my plight? One of them will surely come to my rescue."

"I hope you may be right, but they have husbands to consider, and the countess is increasing."

"I know, I know. But Chastity and Alex will understand. Didn't they buy that estate in Hampshire for the purpose of putting distance between them and Mother?"

"Yes, but, Sincerity, they have the children to occupy their time. You won't fare any better with them than you are here."

"Oh, Cobbie, please do not add to my distress. I must believe that one of my sisters will have pity on me. They just can't let me down."

"But how did you send the letters? Surely your father never agreed to frank them for you."

"Well, no, but there are ways."

"Sincerity, surely you didn't use his stamp without his permission!" demanded the scandalized companion.

"And why shouldn't I? Papa would have agreed, had

I asked him. I just didn't wish to bother him with such a trivial matter," she said, turning sullen.

"Sincerity Hartford, how could you be so deceitful?" asked Miss Cobb.

"Please don't scold, Cobbie," she entreated. "It has been so terrible here, buried in the country while all the world is in London for the Season. I realize now I went about things in the wrong way."

"Went about what the wrong way?" asked Miss Cobb.

"I allowed my suitors to believe I would welcome an offer. I should have discouraged them before they approached Papa. It would have been a simple thing to do. Some social faux pas that would put them off of me."

"Your mother would have discovered that in no time. Don't you remember when Tranquility tried to do something like that?"

Sincerity sighed. Cobbie was right. Her mother always discovered her little intrigues.

"So why don't you make the best of it and finish that tapestry you started last year?" suggested Miss Cobb.

"I just can't, Cobbie! How can I concentrate on anything? I have never been so bored in my entire life!"

"Well, you won't be bored any longer," said Lady Hartford, sweeping into the room, a vision in pale blue and lemon yellow.

"Why is that, Mother?" asked Sincerity warily.

Lady Hartford stopped in front of her daughter and allowed two letters to drop into her lap. Sincerity's heart sank to her shoes as she recognized her own handwriting and her two sisters' names and directions.

"Well you may gasp, young lady, begging your sisters to rescue you from me!" said her mother, her lips tightly pursed. "You have left me no choice, Sincerity. I have written to your great-aunt in Bath."

"Aunt Prudence? But why?"

"Because I wash my hands of you. Perhaps she will

be able to turn you into a lady. At least in Bath, you will not be able to disgrace yourself among my friends!"

"But, Mother, no one goes to Bath anymore except the old and infirm!"

"And the incorrigible!" exclaimed her mother.

# TWO

Sir Simon McKendrick waved until the newlywed couple's carriage disappeared from sight. The servants by his side drifted away, leaving only the old housekeeper who had practically raised Jessie blowing her nose and sniffling quietly.

"Take heart, Mrs. Tifton. She's in good hands," he said, throwing an arm around the old woman and giving her a squeeze.

"I know, sir, but I'm going t' miss the lass. Won't be th' same around the house without Miss Jessie. And you'll be leaving on the morrow."

"For a short time. As for Jessie, only think, Mrs. Tifton, in a year or two when she comes for a visit, she may bring a babe with her for you to spoil."

"Oh, get along with you, naughty boy," she said, shaking her head and returning to the house.

Still smiling, Simon set out for the old stone chapel that stood in the woods beyond the well-kept grounds of the keep. His gait was brisk, and the kilt he wore swirled around his legs with each step. He had not bothered to change to his heavy shoes and was glad the lawn was free of stones.

The old iron gate swung open noiselessly; everything on the estate was kept in excellent order, with or without his presence. His people loved the place as much as he did, and they took pride in their home. He passed the building, strolling through the headstones that marked the lives of centuries of McKendrick ancestors.

He stopped in front of the simple square marker, reading the words, as always, and feeling again the painful emptiness. He knelt on one knee and bowed his head for a moment.

"Eight years, my love, and I still miss you. I know I should be glad you and the baby are together, but it's very difficult being here alone. I try not to think of the child. She'd be such a bonnie lass now, with green eyes like you and dark hair."

He plucked a stray weed from the ground and cleared his throat before continuing. "I'm going to go away again. Not like last time. Last time I had the war to help me set aside my loneliness. That's the problem, you see. When I came home, it was as if everything was fresh all over again. I thought the pain would fade with time, but it didn't. When I got home, there was a part of me that still expected you to come out of the house and throw your arms around my neck."

Simon rose, swiping at a lone tear before he concluded matter-of-factly, "I'll only be gone for a month or two. It won't work a miracle, of course, but I promised Jessie, you see. Anyway, I leave tomorrow, my love, but I shan't forget. I'll never forget."

If Sincerity Hartford was anything, she was persistent. But this time, her constant moaning had no effect on her mother or father; it only served to irritate her companion, Miss Cobb. In fact, the mild-mannered lady was so fed up with her charge that she began to snap back at her.

"Would you like me to read to you, my dear?" she asked on the eighteenth day of their country exile.

"No-o-o-o, that's all right."

"Would you like to go for a walk on the beach?"

"No-o-o-o, the sight of that vast emptiness, knowing that Tranquility is somewhere on the other side of it, and free, only serves to sadden me," Sincerity replied, heaving a sigh.

"Oh, for goodness sake, Sincerity, must you be so annoying? If you are bored, why not find something constructive to do? I'm certain there is mending to do, your embroidery, or you could even help Cook with the baking."

"Ugh! You know I hate to sew, and the last time I helped Cook with the baking, she threatened to put me in the oven!"

"Then make up some baskets for the poor. I'm sure the vicar's wife could tell you what is needed," she said, knowing Mrs. Ames could use the help.

As the mistress of the largest estate around, Lady Hartford should have been the one who cared for the parish poor, but her ladyship never occupied herself with such charitable matters, nor had she trained her daughters to do so.

As Miss Cobb expected, Sincerity moaned, "No-o-o-o. Visiting the poor is so very tedious."

"Then I have done with you, Miss Selfish. If you do not care to help yourself, then you may keep your own company!"

"Oh, Cobbie, please do not be angry with me. I'm sorry to be such a bear, truly I am. It is just the thought of going to Bath to visit Aunt Prudence. I have only met her once, when I was a child, and she absolutely terrified me!" said Sincerity, a single tear escaping from her blue eyes and trickling down her porcelain cheek.

Miss Cobb threw her arms around her charge, giving her a bracing squeeze. "There, there, pet. That was years ago. Your great-aunt has no doubt mellowed with time. Perhaps she didn't like children. Some people don't, you know. But now you are all grown-up, a well-mannered young lady. I'm sure you and your aunt will get along famously."

"Perhaps," said Sincerity doubtfully. "I do hope Mother will allow you to accompany me."

"Of course she will. I heard her tell your father that she wouldn't want your attendance on your aunt to be a burden since your aunt is likely to leave you something in her will."

"Really? I had no idea," said Sincerity, cheered by this news. "Do you suppose it will be enough for us to set up house somewhere?"

"I couldn't say, and I suggest you keep this news to yourself."

"But if she did . . ."

"Sincerity, you cannot count on anything from this aunt whom you hardly know."

"I shan't, but it does give me hope. I promise I will be the most agreeable houseguest Great-Aunt Prudence has ever had!"

Considerably cheered, Sincerity rose and went to the kitchen to help Cook with the baking. The skeptical cook allowed her to knead the bread, watching her for several minutes before grunting in satisfaction and returning to the apple tart she was making.

Humming cheerfully, Sincerity's energetic kneading soon had flour all over herself and the floor. Looking at the cook anxiously, she stammered, "I'm sorry, Cookie. I will clean it up. I promise."

"There, there, child. You're doing a fine job of the kneading. A little flour on the floor is to be expected. Now, just put it in the pan and smear it with a bit of butter."

When this task was complete, Sincerity asked, "Is there anything else to do?"

"Well, I do have a basket of goodies for old Mrs. Brown," said Cook doubtfully.

"I'd be happy to take it to her," replied Sincerity, surprising herself as much as the servant by her unusual offer.

"Thank you, miss. That will allow the maids to continue with their cleaning."

"Just let me change. I'll be back down in a trice," she replied, her off-key humming floating after her as she made her way up the back stairs to her room.


Sincerity's light mood began to fade as she made her way back home after delivering Mrs. Brown's basket. The sight of the weathered stone manor house, the thought of her mother waiting within, was enough to lower anyone's spirits.

When she drove the dogcart into the stable yard, she encountered James, who was carrying the mail to the house. He greeted her and stopped to stroke the nose of the ancient cob pulling her cart.

James was wed to Cook's daughter and had worked at Hartford Manor all his life. He was perhaps ten years her senior, but he seemed so old and wise. When she was younger, she had trailed behind him in the stables like a puppy. That was before the horse had kicked her, breaking her arm. Now, she avoided all the horses except old Brownie, but she was still on the best of terms with James.

"Good morning, James. How are Jane and the twins? Are they over that little illness?"

"Yes, miss, they're fine now. We're hoping the baby won't come down with it."

"Oh, I hope not, too. She's only two months old, isn't she?" He nodded in response, and Sincerity gave him her most winning smile and asked, "If that's the mail, I'll take it into the house for you, James."

"Thank you, miss. That would save me a trip."

Sincerity detoured through the gardens, putting off entering the house as long as possible. She could smell the bread that she had helped make and was tempted to go into the kitchens for a hot slice, but her steps faltered, and she sat down on a stone bench in the rose arbor. Placing the mail on the seat, she stretched, an unladylike, catlike movement that would have given her mother a case of the vapors had she been a witness to it.

Several moments passed before Sincerity sighed and gathered up the mail. Suddenly she frowned, spying an envelope with her name on it. She held it in her hand, turning it this way and that, puzzling over the unfamiliar, spidery hand.

It had been sent to the London town house and then forwarded to Folkestone. It had her father's name on it, too, above her name. Her mother would be furious if she opened it. It was very probably the summons from her great-aunt.

Sincerity's gaze traveled around the garden, flitting toward the house, but the rose arbor hid her from view. She tore open the envelope, her eyes widening with each word she read. When she had finished, she sat back, forcing herself to breathe evenly while her mind flew through all the possibilities.

Great-Aunt Prudence—dead! The words danced before her, taunting her with lost hopes. Suddenly the idea of going to Bath—even to an aunt she barely remembered—getting away from her despotic mother, and meeting new people seemed like a veritable paradise. And here it was, snatched from her.

The tears that sparkled in Sincerity's blue eyes were for herself, for the might-have-beens.

"Sincerity!" cried her mother, her voice sharp with impatience. "Where is that girl?"

"I'm here, Mother," called Sincerity, tucking the letter into her bodice and wiping her eyes on her sleeve before stepping into view. "I'm just back from visiting Mrs. Brown."

"James told me he handed you the morning post. Is that it?" she demanded, pointing at the letters in her daughter's hand. "You know I am expecting a reply from Great-Aunt Prudence."

"There was nothing from her," said Sincerity, a little too suddenly, for her mother's gaze narrowed, and they stared at each other for a moment before Sincerity dropped her gaze. "That is, I didn't see anything that appeared to be from her."

Lady Hartford appeared satisfied for she turned and strolled away, sifting through the envelopes. Sincerity felt the stiff paper against her breasts and wondered how she had managed to remain upright. Going through the kitchens, she forced a tremulous smile for the cook; then she turned and fled to the sanctuary of her room.

She pulled out the letter and began reading again. It was from her great-aunt's solicitor and contained the requisite polite words of condolence. What followed was a great deal of information about property and servants that Sincerity only skimmed through.

She arrived at the last paragraph, skimmed it, then reread it slowly, her heart beginning to beat erratically. All of the property, the servants, the—gulp!—money that her miserly aunt had managed to accumulate through eighty years of life were to go to her only unwed great-niece, her namesake, Miss Sincerity Prudence Hartford!


"Hartford, I do believe I will write to Aunt Prudence again. Perhaps I didn't convey the urgency of my request in my last letter," said Divinity Hartford at dinner that evening.

"Hm? Oh, yes, it certainly couldn't hurt," he replied, reluctantly returning his attention to the present. "I think I'm going to go up to London tomorrow morning. Did you want to go with me, Divinity?" he asked politely.

"I would love to," she said, raising a brow at her daughter before she continued, "but I cannot leave right now. If you might delay your journey for a few days . . ."

"Very well, but not past Thursday. If you haven't heard from Aunt Prudence by then, you'll just have to stay behind."

"Of course," came the curt reply.

"I can certainly supervise Sincerity if you wish to go to London, my lady," said Miss Cobb quietly, apologetically.

"No, Miss Cobb. She has a way of wrapping you about her little finger."

"Mother, I am not a child," said Sincerity.

"No, you most certainly are not," retorted her mother. "You are three and twenty and well past the age to need a chaperon of any sort, if only you were wed."

"Ladies, ladies, let us turn the topic," said Lord Hartford. "This is hardly the sort of dinner conversation that will help the digestion. Didn't I see a letter from your old friend Lady Humphries in the post today, Divinity?"

"Yes, she was telling me all about her sister's daughter, who made such an advantageous match early in the Season. It seems they are to wed at the end of the month."

"And how is Lord Humphries?" asked Lord Hartford hurriedly.

"He is sickly as ever. I declare, Hartford, I can't recall a time when that man . . ."

After the interminable dinner, Sincerity was forced to play the pianoforte for an hour while her mother dozed and Miss Cobb and Lord Hartford played a game of chess. Then the tea tray arrived, and she poured out. Finally, she was able to excuse herself and flee to her room for the night.

She allowed her abigail to dress her for bed and then sent her away curtly. Marnie was apt to be chatty, and she was in no mood for chatter tonight!

The plan that had been simmering in her head had finally taken shape at dinner, when her mother had refused to allow her to remain at home with only Cobbie for company. She could see the years stretching before her with her mother constantly hovering over her shoulder. The picture was intolerable!

But what could she do? What could she possibly do?

Sincerity retrieved the letter from behind the heavy wardrobe and scurried back to bed. Leaning toward the candle, she slowly perused the letter for the fourth or fifth time. Though she didn't understand all of the legal terms, there was no doubt about her being the only heir to what seemed to be a considerable estate. She didn't understand all the bits about shares and bonds, either, but she did recognize that the solicitor wanted to know what to do with the house, indicating that he would keep all the servants there until such time as he heard from Lord Hartford.

Papa, not her. She didn't count. She wouldn't reach her majority for almost two years, so she couldn't possibly make decisions regarding her property, her inheritance. Life was so unfair!

But she didn't despair. Sincerity Hartford had learned through the years that if the facts were not what one wanted or needed, one simply altered the facts.

She rose, carrying the candelabra to the small writing desk near the window. She sharpened a pen and drew out a sheet of her father's best stationery, the paper with his name engraved on top that she had given him last Boxing Day.

After dipping the pen in ink, she wrote with bold strokes:

*Dear Mr. Cooper,*
*While I am, of course, delighted to learn of my youngest daughter's inheritance, I am unable to come to Bath personally to tend to legal matters. My wife and I will be attending my other daughter, the Countess of Beaulieu, in France for the next month, awaiting the birth of our third grandchild. Therefore, I am sending my daughter Sincerity and her very competent companion to take over the property. This is perhaps a little irregular, but you may have all confidence in Miss Cobb, a regular tartar of a female, who is quite capable of overseeing the transfer of deeds and such. My daughter is of a delicate nature, and after consulting with her physician, we have decided the fresh air and waters in Bath might be just the thing to put her on her feet again.*
*They will arrive in Bath within the week. Please do all you can to make them comfortable. In my absence, I rely on you and Miss Cobb completely.*
*Hartford*

A nervous giggle escaped Sincerity, and she swung around, staring at the closed door for a moment to make certain no one would discover her. After carefully copying the solicitor's direction on the envelope, she took out another sheet of stationery, this time choosing a pale yellow paper with no identifying marks.

She repaired the point on the pen and once again began to write, allowing her hand to quiver from time to time as she formed the spidery text to imitate the shaky handwriting of an older woman.

She reread her efforts and nodded. That should do it. Her great-aunt would never have spent too much time on the niceties. The letter inviting her great-niece Sincerity and "Miss Cobb, that companion of hers" to Bath was short and to the point. There was a hint of condescending arrogance that she, Great-Aunt Prudence, would accomplish what Divinity hadn't been able to do—find a husband for Sincerity.

One final touch, she thought with a smile, adding a line about not wanting her house in Bath filled with countless nieces. That should keep her mother at home!

Sincerity waited until the household was silent before slipping downstairs to her father's study. She had watched Tranquility do it many times, writing letters to the suitors her parents didn't quite approve of. Still, that was one thing. Being the one franking the letters was quite another. Her hand shook as she placed the stamp on the letter to her mother.

The main thing, of course, was to go to Folkestone to post the letters instead of trying to slip them into her father's mail. That was how her mother had discovered her letters to her sisters. This time, she would make certain that didn't happen.

Slipping the letters into the pocket of her wrapper, Sincerity climbed the stairs and hurried back to her room to complete her sleepless night.

"The most extraordinary thing, Hartford, in today's post," said her mother, looking up from the letter she was reading. "Great-Aunt Prudence has invited Sincerity to Bath. . . ."

"That's good news," murmured her husband, glancing at his wife over the top of his newspaper.

"Yes, but she insists that only Miss Cobb accompany Sincerity. I had no idea she even knew about Miss Cobb. I don't think I mentioned her in my letter."

Sincerity bit at her lower lip and forced herself to keep her eyes on the needlework that was in her lap.

"You must have done. Besides, Miss Cobb has been with us for so many years, her name was bound to come up from time to time."

"Yes, I suppose that is it," said Lady Hartford.

"So, when can you be ready to go to Bath, young lady?" asked her father.

Her mother replied for her. "I don't see why we can't leave on Wednesday."

"We?"

"Yes, we. Your father and I are returning to London for the remainder of the Season. You and Miss Cobb will accompany us there before journeying on to Bath."

Sincerity breathed a sigh of relief and smiled, making her mother frown.

"And let me warn you, Sincerity, one word from your great-aunt, and that will be it. You'll remain here at Hartford Manor for the rest of your days. Do you understand?"

"Yes, Mother. I promise I'll be good."

"You had better be. I shall be writing to your Aunt Prudence regularly for reports on your behavior."

"Yes, Mother," whispered Sincerity, hiding her gleeful heart by keeping her head bowed in a semblance of maidenly modesty.

The journey to London was anything but comfortable under her mother's keen scrutiny. And though they were weary before they left, Sincerity and Miss Cobb could not keep from smiling as they set out on the road to Bath.

They spent two nights at posting inns. On the third morning, when Sincerity greeted her companion for breakfast, she found it difficult to eat. Her usually hearty appetite fled as she contemplated revealing her deception to dear Miss Cobb. The genteel lady would be horrified by her charge's duplicitous actions. But she had to be told. She had to be won over before they arrived in Bath.

"You are very quiet this morning, Sissie," said Miss Cobb. "You've hardly touched your scones, and they are quite as good as Cook's, light and buttery."

"I'm sure they are wonderful, Cobbie, but there is something I must discuss with you, something I must tell you."

The former governess blanched and set her teacup down with a clatter. She knew that pitiful tone; it foretold some piece of disturbing news. Not for the first time, she wished she had wed that dull farmer's boy when she was a girl, instead of running away to become a governess.

Miss Cobb squared her shoulders. In martyred tones, she said, "I am waiting."

"Great-Aunt Prudence is not going to be at home to greet us when we arrive."

The scones Miss Cobb had just been extolling dropped to the pit of her stomach like stones. "She is out of town?" she asked hopefully.

Sincerity shook her head. "No, not out of town. She is . . . dead."

Miss Cobb slumped in her chair, a posture she would never have allowed herself except under dire circumstances. Sincerity wet her handkerchief in the cool ale and began dabbing it on Miss Cobb's wrists. Her companion waved her away, picked up her teacup, and drained the hot liquid without another word. She stared, her mouth gaping. She shook her head, looked up again, and once again shook her head.

"Say something," whispered Sincerity with a nervous giggle.

"What is there to say? Have you lost your mind? Are you ready for Bedlam at such an early age?"

"No, I have not lost my mind. Rather, I have found it. Cobbie, only think! You and I, in Bath, without anyone telling us what to do or say! What a glorious time we shall have!"

"Glorious time? You are mad! What are you going to do for money? Have you thought about that? Where will we stay? What will we do for food?"

Sincerity giggled and whispered, "I'll pay for everything!"

"You? You can't even make it to quarter day before you are wheedling more pin money out of your father. And believe me, my girl, he won't look favorably on you after you have pulled this hen-witted scheme!"

"Cobbie, calm down. People are beginning to stare," whispered Sincerity, pasting a smile on her features as she looked around the inn parlor where several parties of travelers were breaking their fasts.

"I'm sorry, Sincerity. I have been your champion throughout, but you have gone too far this time. How you can believe we can manage to keep body and soul together in Bath is beyond me. We will starve! Worse yet, we will be out in the streets in a week!"

"Well, I did leave out one small detail, my dearest Cobbie. I'm an heiress."

"Your father is hardly likely to settle anything on you when he is still . . ."

"Not Papa, silly. Great-Aunt Prudence." She opened her reticule and pulled out the solicitor's letter. "I am her only heir, and from what I read in this letter, I can buy and sell half of London, if I wish."

Miss Cobb took the envelope. "It is addressed to your father!" she observed in hushed tones.

"But my name is on the envelope as well. Just read it."

"I really shouldn't," she said, handing the envelope back to her charge who grimaced, pulled out the worn pieces of paper, and began to read aloud. After a sentence or two, Miss Cobb extracted the letter from Sincerity's fingers and read it in silence.

"Well, you were right about one thing. You are an heiress. Your father has some shares in this company she mentions. He even purchased some for me, and they've done quite well. And then there are the properties."

"Quite," said Sincerity, sitting back and smiling happily.

"But Sincerity, this is hardly going to make any difference. You are not of age, just as the solicitor says, so your father has control of everything."

"Well, I forgot to mention that Papa wrote a reply to this Mr. Cooper, informing him about our arrival."

"He did?" came the incredulous reply.

"Well, let us say the solicitor received a letter written and signed by Lord Hartford."

"Oh, Sincerity, you didn't!"

"Yes, I did, and I would do it again!" she snapped.

Miss Cobb reread the letter, shaking her head from time to time. Then she frowned anew.

"What about the letter from your Great-Aunt Prudence? The solicitor says she was ill for a week and then died. Surely she wouldn't have invited . . . us . . . to Bath. Oh, Sincerity, not the letter your mother received, too!"

"I'm afraid so," said Sincerity, her grin robbing her words of any semblance of remorse.

"We shall both go to hell," whispered Miss Cobb, who had been raised by a devout vicar with strong Methodist tendencies.

"Not before we have a splendid time in Bath!" declared Sincerity, rising and pulling her companion to her feet. "Come along, Miss Cobb. We are wasting time, and we have a city to conquer."

\* \* \*

"Let's go over it one more time," said Miss Cobb, her voice quivering wearily as their hired coach reached the outskirts of Bath.

"All right. I am feeling poorly, having been sick for some time. You are in charge of everything, from paying the coachmen to greeting the solicitor."

"Well, the first part of that is true enough. Your father did entrust me with the money for the journey. But why do you have to be ill?"

"Not ill, just recovering. That's why I didn't go to France with my parents."

"But your parents are in London!" complained the straitlaced Miss Cobb, wiping her brow with her handkerchief.

"But not according to the letter I sent Mr. Cooper," said Sincerity. "For one thing, I want them to be too far away for him to be able to write to them and verify what he has already been told."

"Yes, yes, that's right. I forgot. Oh, Sincerity, I fear I have no head for intrigue. I shall never be able to remember all the twists of this tale."

"It's perfectly simple. Mother and Father went to France to be with Tranquility during her confinement."

"As if they would," murmured Miss Cobb.

"Well, yes, but Mr. Cooper needn't know they would never do such a thing. You have accompanied me to Bath, hoping the sea air and waters will bring me back to my former robust self, which they will in no time." This last earned her a quizzical look from her companion, and she sighed and continued patiently, "Of course I will get better quickly. The last thing I want to do is spend my time in Bath, my time of freedom, shut up in the house languishing like an invalid!"

"Of course. Go on."

"Until I am better, you will take care of the solicitor and all of his questions. You will tell him that you will keep Lord Hartford informed personally so there will be no need for him to write to Papa."

"You really do think of everything," marveled Miss Cobb.

"I have to. I want this to be a success, and I want both of us to be able to relax and enjoy ourselves."

"For tomorrow we die," said the companion gloomily.

"For tomorrow, after taking care of business with the solicitor, you and I will have a shopping trip on the Milsom Street like you have never seen. And Cobbie, once I have control of my money, you will stay with me forever," said Sincerity fiercely. "You know I couldn't do without you, don't you?"

Miss Cobb patted her charge's hand and said, "You are a complete scamp and a hoyden, but I will not desert you—ever."

"Good, because I believe we have arrived."

"Oh, no!" breathed her companion.

"Remember your role; you are the dragon!" whispered Sincerity as the door to the coach opened.

"We're here, ladies," said the coachman, waiting to hand them down personally. One of the grooms her father had hired for the journey was already carrying their bandboxes and portmanteaus to the door and beating a loud tattoo.

"Thank you, sir. You did very well," said Miss Cobb, handing him several coins. "Come along, my dear," she added, putting her arm around her charge and coaxing her toward the door.

The coachman watched for a moment, scratching his head at the state of the formerly robust young lady who had started the journey. Then he climbed back on the box and turned the coach around, heading for the nearest inn.

"That went well," whispered Miss Cobb, turning pale as the door swung open on its well-oiled hinges.

"Yes?" asked the starchiest butler they had ever seen.

His gray hair was neatly trimmed, and his suit was immaculate. On his arm, he wore a black band. Drat! thought Sincerity. She should be wearing one, too.

She realized suddenly that Miss Cobb had already forgotten her role as dragon, and she moaned, leaning heavily on her companion's arm.

"Oh, yes, hello," squeaked Miss Cobb, starting to enter the hallway. The tall butler stepped onto the threshold, blocking their entrance.

"May I help you, madam?"

"This is Miss Sincerity Hartford, and I am her companion, Miss Cobb. This is Miss Prudence Granville's residence, is it not?" she managed to say.

"Yes, it is, but my mistress said nothing about expecting some young miss and a governess, and I don't recall any Hartfords. Good day, madam." He took one step back and closed the door in their faces.

Sincerity put an arm around Miss Cobb for support.

# THREE

The dragon suddenly came to life, thrusting her foot into the aperture and pushing the door open once again.

Sincerity could feel Miss Cobb straighten her spine. From her vantage point, she peeked up to see Miss Cobb lift her nose to the same degree as the toplofty butler's.

Her eyes snapping, she declared, "I daresay that is because your mistress is no longer alive, sirrah. But this is Miss Prudence Granville's house, and this young lady is her great-niece, Miss Sincerity Prudence Hartford. Surely Mr. Cooper warned you of our arrival."

Still he did not move. Only his nose reached new heights.

"I have received no messages from Mr. Cooper."

Miss Cobb's shoulders drooped. She was in danger of losing her resolve and that, Sincerity knew, would spell disaster!

"Oh, Cobbie, I . . ." With an audible sigh, Sincerity swooned.

"Now see what you've done! Well, don't just stand there like a looby. Help me get her into the house!"

The startled butler snapped his fingers and a hulking footman leaped forward and swept the petite Sincerity into his arms as if she were a feather. Sincerity found herself placed gently on a settee in a cold, darkened parlor.

"It's like an ice house in here," said Miss Cobb. "Light the fire, my good man, and then open the curtains."

"Yes, ma'am," said the young footman, tearing his eyes away from the limp figure on the sofa and doing as he was bid.

Miss Cobb pulled a vial out of her reticule and waved it under Sincerity's nose.

She sputtered a cough and opened her eyes, blinking rapidly before closing them again and saying in die-away tones, "Where are we, Miss Cobb?"

"Where we should be," said Miss Cobb, looking over her shoulder at the butler, daring him to dispute her words. "We'll soon have you tucked up in bed, won't we, Mr. . . .?"

"Really, madam," began the butler, but Miss Cobb rose and stared him down until he said through thin, pursed lips, "Sam, tell the maids to make up two of the guest chambers for these, uh, ladies."

"Right away, Mr. Crispin."

"The best guest chambers," added Miss Cobb.

Crispin nodded.

"Dearest Cobbie, you were magnificent, absolutely magnificent!" declared Sincerity, hugging her weak-kneed friend fiercely as soon as the door to her chamber had closed.

"Sincerity, I thought I would faint! Whatever would we have done if that horrid man hadn't let us enter?"

"It wasn't going to happen! And even if he had refused, it would only have been temporary. A quick visit to Mr. Cooper's office, and we would soon have routed the irritating Crispin!"

"I'm too old for these sorts of shenanigans," moaned Miss Cobb, sinking onto the bench in front of the glass.

"You are no such thing!" declared Sincerity. "You are a trooper, a regular trooper!"

"I don't feel like a trooper; I feel weary and worn."

"Then go to your room, Cobbie, and rest. I'll ring for a tea tray."

"I couldn't eat a thing."

"Nonsense. You know you'll feel much better once you've had your cup of tea. Come on. I'll play the role of your abigail."

"Oh, no, not another role," groaned Miss Cobb.

"Very well, no more roles. You have a little lie down."

"I don't think I can," protested the companion, allowing her charge to guide her through the connecting door to her own chamber.

"How lovely," said Sincerity, "and in your favorite color, too."

Miss Cobb lifted her head and looked at the well-appointed room with its sitting area and huge oak bed, which was hung with rose-colored drapes and covered by a pale pink counterpane. The bed called to her, and she allowed Sincerity to help her undress before climbing onto the soft feather bed.

"Perhaps a little nap would help," she said, smiling up at her charge who pulled the pink cover up under her friend's chin.

"Rest well, Cobbie. I'll look in on you in an hour."

"Thank you, my dear."

Sincerity returned to her own room, a slight smile curving her lips. She rather liked being the one in charge. All her life, she had sat back and let others run everything. It hadn't really been her idea, she reflected; her twin sister had always insisted on being the ringleader. Now, however, she was her own mistress and could decide what she wanted to do and when. What a heady feeling!

She wandered to the window and stared out at the

small, neat garden below. She imagined herself sitting among the flowers, a tall, strong man by her side. His face was shadowy, but his arm was around her waist, and she felt safe and warm.

With a sigh, Sincerity turned away and pulled the rope. The huge footman appeared instantly, and she guessed he had been waiting for her summons.

"Your name is Sam, isn't it?" she asked shakily, remembering her role of invalid.

"Yes, miss. Did you need something?"

"Yes, Sam, I'm feeling rather peckish. Do you think the cook might be able to make up a tea tray for me?"

"I'm sure he can, miss. I'll be back quick as th' cat can lick its whiskers," he said, hurrying toward the servant's stairs.

An excellent ally, thought Sincerity. She turned her thoughts to her surroundings and crossed the dark, paneled hall, opening the door opposite hers. It was dark, too, but it was well kept without a hint of any musty smell. She crossed the floor and opened the heavy drapes before turning to inspect the huge bedchamber.

"My goodness," she murmured. "It must run the entire width of the house."

On the left, the room contained the requisite bed and dressing table, but it didn't end there. There was a large, comfortable sitting area on the right with a second fireplace. Beyond that, there was a wall of bookcases from floor to ceiling, stuffed with books and small knickknacks. In the corner was a sturdy writing desk, the sort one would expect to see in a study or library, not in a bedroom. Pillars here and there served as divisions between the various areas.

The noise of a passing carriage drew Sincerity's attention away from the chamber and back to the window that overlooked the street. Her heart leaped at the scene beyond. She saw two older gentlemen passing the time of day in the small park across the street. Strolling down the sidewalk was a stern-faced matron with three chattering young ladies, all dressed in the first stare. An open landau passed and drew up beside the matron, the occupant leaning forward and saying something.

Sincerity threw open the window, then stepped back when all eyes turned toward the house. She waited for them to resume their conversation before she closed the window and hurried back to her room.

"Oh, there you are," said Sam, turning from the small table where he had just deposited a silver tray laden with a tempting collation and a sturdy teapot.

"I just wanted to see what was across the way. It's an unusual room, isn't it?" commented Sincerity, passing the servant and sitting down beside the tray.

"Yes, miss. Miss Granville would stay in there for days at a time, and only Mr. Crispin and her old maid were allowed inside to serve her."

"That was my aunt's room?"

"Yes, miss. Did you need anything else?"

"No, nothing. Thank you, Sam," she said, smiling at the tall young man. When she had earned his trust, she would ask him about this mysterious relative of hers who had managed to live her life exactly as she pleased.

After satisfying her hunger, Sincerity wandered around the cheery chamber, picking up a porcelain shepherdess, touching the soft yellow draperies around the bed, leaning against the windowsill, and staring out at the garden.

She slipped across the hall and began a thorough examination of her late aunt's bookshelves, smiling when she discovered among the travel guides and books of poetry, a wide range of novels, including some of her favorites. She selected one and carried it to the window, which had a comfortable, cushioned seat attached to it. She settled onto the blue velvet cushion and opened the book, but her attention drifted to the scene below.

Across the street, two small boys were throwing a stick for a scruffy little dog while their nanny sat on a bench watching over them. A brightly painted wagon rattled down the street, carrying several pieces of furniture destined, no doubt, for one of the elegant houses.

"Life is passing me by," whispered Sincerity. She glanced back at the book, snapped it closed, and hurried across the hall to her own chamber. Quickly, she changed her gown for one of her smart carriage dresses and put on a matching bonnet.

She peeked out the door, wishing she had asked Sam where the back stairs led. She hesitated only a moment before choosing the servants' stairs as the least likely route to lead to the disapproving butler. She pushed open the door at the foot of the stairs and glanced around the small dining area set aside for the servants.

Sam, who was busy polishing silverware, glanced up and jumped to his feet. Sincerity put her finger to her lips.

"Sam, is there a way out of the garden?" she whispered.

"Out of the garden?"

"Yes, you know, to the streets?"

"Yes, miss. Go straight through, and when you get to the back gate, you turn left."

"Thank you," she said, giving him a smile before scurrying to the door.

"I'm glad you're feeling better, miss, but . . . I, uh . . . Do you want me to go with you?"

Sincerity paused. In London, she had always taken her maid to preserve the proprieties. Here, she hadn't considered it necessary. But while she wasn't known in Bath, she didn't want to shock any of its social leaders by appearing without so much as an attendant.

"I don't want you to get into trouble with Mr. Crispin, Sam," she protested mildly.

"Oh, I won't. I'll just put this away," he said, gathering up the silver and putting it into a drawer. "I can finish it later, miss."

"Thank you, Sam. I do want to go exploring, but I didn't want to trouble my companion. She's still resting."

"You can ask me anytime, miss," he said, opening the door for her.

"That's good to know, Sam," she replied.

The young footman led her through the garden and to the nearest street. Sincerity found it impossible to refrain from grinning ear to ear. Her heart sang a constant refrain; "I'm free! I'm free!"

"Where did you want to go, miss?" asked Sam.

"I want to go to the shops, Sam. I just want to see all the people and look in the windows!" Sincerity peered up at him self-consciously and admitted, "I know you must think me mad, Sam, but I am so excited to be here in Bath. Home was not very pleasant, I'm afraid. My mother . . . Well, never mind that. But do you think we could go to the shops?"

"We can do anything you like, Miss Hartford. Now, so we can keep things properlike, I'll walk behind you, but I'll tell you which way to turn as we go."

"How clever of you!" said Sincerity, leading the way as he directed. When there was no one close by, she conversed with the young footman, finding conversation with the servant much more comfortable than with a man of her own station.

"How old are you, Sam?"

"I'm nineteen, miss. I'm just big for my age."

"And I'm just small for mine," she said, with a trill of laughter. "I am three and twenty, and according to certain people, should already have a husband and a nursery full of children."

"My uncle always says people do what they are meant to do," replied Sam.

"Why, I think your uncle a very smart man."

"Oh, Uncle Charles is wonderful smart like that. Just turn right at the next corner, miss, and you'll be on Milsom Street, where all the gentry come to shop."

Sincerity turned the corner and then stopped, enthralled by the bustling scene before her. It was nothing like the streets in London where one might or might not see acquaintances. There was an intimacy about the people as they strolled and talked, stopping every few minutes to greet someone new. The gentlemen's somber hues mingled pleasingly with the ladies' gaily colored gowns, like the rich soil that held spring flowers. It was utterly charming.

And the shops! There appeared to be every sort she could hope for.

"Is that a bookstore?" she whispered over her shoulder.

"Yes, miss. I used to come here often to fetch new books for Miss Granville."

"I must go inside," said Sincerity, crossing the street. She paused when she entered the building, closing her eyes and breathing deeply the scent of leather bindings and musty papers. So enraptured was she that she failed to see the gentleman, his arms full of books, making his way through the doors. They collided with a decided thud that sent his books flying.

"Oh, please excuse me, miss. I didn't see you there!" he said politely, his Scottish accent pleasing to the ear.

Sincerity felt herself set to rights by strong, yet gentle hands. Her eyes traveled past a broad chest, across a whittled jaw, and into warm gray eyes. She felt a tremor of excitement. They were smiling eyes that twinkled for her, only for her. The man behind those eyes cleared his throat, and Sincerity colored up, realizing she was staring like a country bumpkin.

"I beg your pardon, sir," she said, her voice shallow

as if she had been running. She looked down at the scattered volumes and yelped, "Let me help you." Retrieving the first one, her eyes widened when she read the title. It was a novel by Minerva Press, one of the books she absolutely loved . . . secretly.

He took it from her, his hand grazing hers. "Thank you, but I can manage, miss. You came to no harm, I trust?"

Sincerity managed a shake of her head though her body was unaccountably trembling. His voice was low and soft, conjuring images of stolen caresses.

"No, no, I am fine," she said airily.

"Good. There, all done," he added, straightening and giving her a special smile. Balancing the books with one hand, he tipped his hat and left the store.

Sincerity stared after those wide shoulders, her cheeks growing ruddy as her gaze dropped lower and took in the plaid kilt and strong calves clad in thick knit stockings. Dragging her eyes away from this unsettling vision, she noted the tawny-gold queue protruding from his hat. He turned suddenly, as if aware of her scrutiny, and she whirled around, stepping outside again and hurrying away in the opposite direction while she willed her breath to return to normal.

"Is anything wrong, miss?" said Sam, practically running to catch up with her.

"Wrong? No, no, I just decided to save the bookstore for tomorrow when Miss Cobb can accompany me. She loves a good book as much as I do."

"Just like my uncle," murmured the servant, falling into step behind her again as her pace returned to normal.

Sincerity didn't enter any other shops, not even when she was sorely tempted by the popular modiste's array of colorful silks draped enticingly in its windows. Determined to keep her reputation shining, she nodded to a few of the ladies, but dropped her gaze demurely when any gentleman bowed.

After she had strolled from one end and back, she told Sam she was satisfied, and they turned toward home. Before they entered the house, she took a coin and handed it to the footman.

"That's not necessary, miss. It was my pleasure to be your guide on your first day here."

"Nevertheless, Sam, you were an excellent and willing guide. It's only right you should receive a small reward. Besides, I'm still not convinced you won't get into trouble with Mr. Crispin. I don't want my only friend in the household turned off without a character," she said earnestly.

"Oh, he might cut up stiff, miss, but he won't turn me off. Me mum's his sister, you see. He's my Uncle Charles, though I'm not to call him that when there's others around t' hear."

"Really? I had no idea," replied Sincerity, entering the house to find the butler, tight-lipped as ever, waiting with his arms folded and a fierce frown on his forehead.

"Good afternoon, miss," he said to her.

"Good afternoon, Crispin," stammered Sincerity. "Your nephew was good enough to accompany me on a short stroll."

"Very good, miss," replied the butler, his face showing no emotion whatsoever.

Sincerity gave Sam a quick smile and hurried past the butler and up the servants' stairs. She hoped Crispin wouldn't be too angry with his nephew. Sam was such an agreeable attendant. He knew his place but was young enough to understand her curiosity.

When she opened her door, Miss Cobb was waiting.

"And where have you been, young lady?" demanded Miss Cobb, reverting to her former role of governess with ease. "I have been up and worrying about you for the past half an hour. Mr. Crispin said he thought you had taken Sam with you, since he was also missing. I could tell he was quite cross, although I know he was at pains to hide his displeasure from me."

Sincerity sniffed and affected a haughty stare. "I'm sure there is nothing wrong with a lady taking a walk in the afternoon, even here in Bath, especially accompanied by a footman."

"But, Sincerity, Sam is hardly more than a boy. You must be very careful in your attitude with him. It wouldn't do for . . ."

"Sam is nineteen years old, hardly likely to consider himself a suitable candidate for my paramour," came the outrageous retort. "Really, Cobbie! Have you ever known me to encourage the attentions of a servant?"

"Well, no," admitted Miss Cobb, flushing with embarrassment at such a possibility.

"Of course not. I have too much respect for them to do so, and, I hope, they have too much respect for me. Now, let us hear no more nonsense. The truth of the matter is, Sam is a very kind young man who wanted to please his mistress."

"Very well, Sincerity. I'm sure you were circumspect. I know you want to keep your reputation here in Bath spotless."

"That should not present a problem. Here, without my mother constantly pushing me to encourage this gentleman or that, I shouldn't be troubled by unwanted offers."

"But what about the other sort, the ones that are wanted?"

"There is no 'other sort,' Cobbie. I have told you frequently that I have no desire to wed."

"You say that now . . ." was Miss Cobb's dubious response.

"Yes, I do, Cobbie. I intend to make Bath my home

for the rest of my life, living here quietly. And you will live here with me."

"I only hope we can," said Miss Cobb doubtfully. "I fear, however, your mother will find out about your great-aunt's demise and descend on us . . ."

"Like the hounds of hell," quoted Sincerity with a shudder. Then her blue eyes began to twinkle, and she added irrepressibly, "Don't worry. I will do what I can to appease my mother's curiosity. As a matter of fact, I think Great-Aunt Prudence should write her niece a letter telling of our arrival and how much she is enjoying our company."

"Oh, no," groaned Miss Cobb.

Sincerity had no trouble getting to sleep that night. The excitement of the day was not sufficient to keep her awake. But in her sleep, she could not control her dreams, and if a certain tall, handsome Scot who read romance novels played a prominent role, her slumbering smile was the only clue.

When she awoke, she smiled anew, dismissing the dream as nonsense. Certainly the gentleman was quite fine-looking, but he read novels, for heaven's sake! What sort of man read novels? He was hardly the sort to build dreams around!

Swinging her feet to the cold floor, she padded to the window and opened the curtains. Rubbing her eyes, she frowned at the sunny day, her unruly thoughts straying once again to that broad chest. More likely, scoffed a cynical voice, the man was married and was buying the novels for his wife.

Sincerity turned from the window and smiled again. Or perhaps the novels were for his sister. Perhaps he had a sister who was too ill to go to the bookstore, and he was buying every novel they had to take to her. Such a kind brother, she thought, smiling dreamily. She would see him again, of course. Bath was too small a place to not meet again. He would explain everything to her, would ask her to come and meet his sister. Together they would read to her. . . .

Sincerity giggled. She was adroit at making up tales to suit her fancy, but this was getting out of hand. Her stomach growled, and she dressed hurriedly without the aid of a maid before hurrying down to the kitchens where a warm fire chased away the morning chill. With her china-blue eyes and dimpled smile, she quickly won over the elderly French cook who pressed a light pastry on his pretty young mistress.

"This is wonderful, Hervé. What do you call it?"

"It is a beignet, mademoiselle. I am glad you like it."

"Oh, I do," said Sincerity, sipping from the cup of sweet coffee he had placed on the table for her. "I have noticed, Hervé, that there aren't any female servants. Why is that?"

"As a rule, Madam did not like them. I never asked why."

"I see. That is most unusual."

"There was one maid, her dresser, but she left when Madam died."

"But she was the only one?"

"*Oui*, Madam. She was accustomed to doing things as she saw fit, mademoiselle. She was of an age when she had only to please herself."

"How wonderful that would be," murmured Sincerity wistfully. She flashed the cook a sad little smile, finished her beignet, and thanked him again before leaving the kitchen.

"Good morning, Hervé," said Crispin, stepping into the room when his young mistress had left.

"Mr. Crispin," said the cook, the smile that had fol-

lowed his mistress out slowly fading. He gave a Gaelic
shrug and returned to his breadmaking.

"What did the young mistress want?" asked the butler,
sitting down at the worn table with a cup of tea.

"Some breakfast," replied the cook.

"What do you make of her?" asked the butler.

Again that shrug, but the cook glanced over his shoulder and said firmly, "I think she is a rather sad young
lady who needs a place where she can become happy."

"Indeed?" murmured the butler.


"Get up, Cobbie. You're going to sleep the day away,"
said Sincerity, striding to the windows and pulling back
the rose-colored curtains.

Miss Cobb, her hair confined by a cap, sat up, rubbing
her eyes. "What time is it?"

"Eleven o'clock," said Sincerity with a giggle. "I have
never known you to sleep so late except when we were
at a ball until dawn. Don't tell me you went out dancing
all night without me!" she teased.

"Of course not," grumbled her companion. "It was
just the journey, I suppose. That, and knowing that this
day would prove very trying."

"Why trying? We will summon Mr. Cooper and soon
have everything made official. Then we can be comfortable."

"I hope you may be right," said Miss Cobb.

While Miss Cobb performed her morning ablutions,
Sincerity returned to the sitting room that divided their
chambers and busied herself pouring a cup of tea for her
friend.

"I had Sam bring up your breakfast, Cobbie," she
called. "It seems we don't have a single maid or abigail
to attend to us, something we must remedy if we are to
ever ring for a cup of chocolate in bed of a morning."

"We certainly must!" exclaimed Miss Cobb, entering the room looking quite youthful in a dressing gown of pale pink. "How extraordinary of your great-aunt. How do you suppose she managed to dress herself, to . . . Well, you know."

"Well, according to Cook, she did have one female servant, an older woman who took care of her in that way. But when my aunt died, the maid left, saying she was going to live with her sister."

"But we must have a maid, and we will tell Mr. Crispin so," said Miss Cobb, a militant gleam in her eyes at the thought of facing off with the starchy butler.

"But one maid in a household of male servants? Is that done?" asked Sincerity.

"Well of course it is, if you say it is. You are the mistress!" said Miss Cobb.

Sincerity still looked doubtful, but she turned her attention to more important matters. "I'll play your maid this morning, Cobbie. I thought we might go to the shops, even though we have no money to spend yet. There is the most wonderful modiste's shop and across the way, there is a bookstore, and . . ."

"That's all well and good, Sincerity, but I think we would be better served if we go to the Pump Room today. I understand that is where everyone, who is anyone, is seen."

"Then the Pump Room it is," came the enthusiastic reply.

Later, carefully dressed and coiffed, the two ladies made their way downstairs. Miss Cobb wore a silk gown of darkest navy that complemented her graying hair. Her skin, porcelain with a hint of pink on each cheek, was smooth and clear and made her dark brown eyes stand out like onyx.

"You look lovely today," pronounced Sincerity. "I

wouldn't be surprised if you didn't have to fight off the suitors yourself!"

"And you are tipping the butter boat over my head, miss," came Miss Cobb's sensible reply, but she smiled brightly all the same.

When they reached the foot of the stairs, Crispin was waiting for them. His half bow held no hint of servitude.

"I have taken the liberty of sending for Mr. Cooper, miss," said the butler, glancing at his visitors' attire.

"Thank you, Crispin," said Sincerity.

"If he should call while we are out, be so good as to tell him we will return by four o'clock," said Miss Cobb.

"You are going out?" he asked, eyeing the duo's ensembles.

"Why, uh, yes, we thought . . ." began Sincerity, losing her confidence under his patent disapproval and reverting to the nervous girl her overbearing mother had reared.

Miss Cobb squeezed her charge's hand and drew herself up to her full height, favoring the servant with a frosty stare worthy of the most terrifying grande dame. "Yes, Mr. Crispin, we are going out. Since you did not bother to consult with Miss Hartford or myself before sending for the solicitor, you will need to explain your mistake to him if he should arrive before we return."

"Well, I . . . Yes, ma'am, I shall." He hurried forward to open the door for them. "Do you ladies require an escort? I could send Sam."

"Yes, thank you, Crispin. We will go ahead, and he can catch us up," replied Miss Cobb, melting a bit and taking Sincerity by the arm. On the threshold, she paused again. "Oh, and Mr. Crispin, we require a maid to serve us. Will you please see about hiring someone?"

"Very good, Miss Cobb," he replied with a slight bow.

Sincerity giggled when the door had closed on them.

"You were wonderful, Cobbie! I do believe you out-haughtied Mr. Crispin!"

"Really, Sincerity, you can't just go about making up words to suit your mood. And as for your comment, I won't deign to respond to it. Ah, here is Sam now."

"Good morning, ladies," he said.

"Good morning, Sam," replied Sincerity. "We want to go to the Pump Room. What is the best way from here?"

"Would have been better to call for the carriage, miss. It's farther than the shops we visited yesterday."

"I have a carriage?" asked Sincerity.

"Oh, yes, miss. A big, old, closed carriage and an open landau. There is also a small gig, miss."

"And are there horses?"

"Yes, though there aren't any hacks for riding. Well, there's one, but I don't count him because he's out to pasture."

"Isn't this wonderful news, Miss Cobb? We have our own transport."

Miss Cobb favored her charge with an indulgent smile. "Wonderful news, indeed, my dear, but we should be off if we're going to walk to this Pump Room."

"Of course. Lead on, Sam," said Sincerity, falling into step behind the footman, linking arms with Miss Cobb.

The Pump Room in Bath was the center of social activity during the day. Old tabbies gathered in clusters here and there, throwing out caustic comments about the younger people in attendance. Hopeful mamas flitted about their charges, young damsels dressed in sprig muslins who fluttered their eyes and their fans. Their quarries hovered nearby: young tulips of fashion and infirm, elderly gentlemen whose lascivious stares roamed over the young ladies as if they were cattle at Tattersall's.

"It's not exactly what I expected," whispered Sincerity, looking down at her fashionable bottle green gown trimmed with gold braid and wishing she had chosen something less dazzling, something that would allow her to blend in with the crowd.

The scene was so very familiar to her with its undercurrent of social maneuvering. By the orchestra, a young man successfully won the attention of a lady from her older suitor. On her left, another young lady playfully rapped a septuagenarian on the arm with her fan. Making the best marriage or alliance: such was the mission behind these actions.

Sincerity felt her stomach twist into a knot. Wasn't this what she was trying to avoid? She had only been fooling herself if she thought someone of her age and social standing could live without such entanglements, even here in Bath.

"I think I want to go home, Cobbie," she whispered.

"But it is such an elegant room, my dear. And look over there. What a charming group of young people they are," said Miss Cobb, directing her gaze toward a group of elegantly clad young ladies who were chatting and laughing. About them stood several young bucks, dressed in subdued tones. "They would fit in just as well in a London drawing room," she added.

"Yes, yes. I am just feeling out of place, not having any acquaintances here. I'm . . . sure . . ."

"What is it, my dear? You've gone suddenly pale," said Miss Cobb in alarm. "Sam, help me get your mistress to that chair by the window."

"Really, Cobbie, I am fine," said Sincerity, shaking off her friend and the servant.

"But what happened? You looked as if you would faint! And now you are quite flushed."

"It's nothing, Miss Cobb, nothing." Sincerity willed her color to return to normal while she gazed around the elegantly appointed room with its shiny chandeliers and large windows. A group of musicians played quietly at one end of the room, but Sincerity only glanced their way.

Between her and the musicians stood the cause of her sudden discomfiture. Today he was dressed in breeches rather than in a kilt, but the broad shoulders and that handsome face were unmistakable. It was the same man she had encountered the previous afternoon on her way into the bookstore, the same handsome, virile man. At the moment, he had removed his hat, and she could see that his long hair was a tawny gold, tied back with the same thin, black ribbon. His strong jaw and cheekbones were etched in her memory. His smiling gray eyes now gazed fondly on the group of young ladies and their elegant swains. He seemed a part of the group, and yet, somehow apart from them.

On the pretext of strolling around the room to study the prints that adorned the walls here and there, Sincerity managed to pass by close enough to overhear snippets of the conversation.

"Simon, settle an argument for us. I say that Miss Lang's eyes are azure blue," said one of the young men, drawing the tall stranger forward to join the group.

"And I say they are violet blue, Major," said another of the young men.

*Simon,* thought Sincerity. *What a lovely name for such a handsome man.* He was leaning toward the blushing young lady in question. Sincerity smiled, then blushed herself when the stranger looked past his waiting audience and met her gaze. With a nod, he smiled at her. Sincerity felt her heart leap up in her breast and do a somersault. She dropped her gaze, and Simon returned his attention to the young lady with flaming red hair.

"I would say they are Mediterranean blue, gentlemen. Do you not recall the color of the Mediterranean Sea when we set sail from Portugal?"

"By Jove," exclaimed one of the young swains. "The major is right! I knew I had seen that color before, Miss Lang. I just couldn't remember where!"

"La, Sir Simon, you'll be turning my head," said the pretty Miss Lang, fluttering her fan in front of her face.

"I only wished to settle a dispute, Miss Lang. It wouldn't do for brothers to fight over the color of a lady's eyes, even a lady as pretty as you," said Sir Simon with a bow. "Now, if you'll excuse me, I must be going."

"But you will be at the assembly Thursday night, won't you, Sir Simon?" asked two of the ladies in unison.

"I wouldn't miss it for the world," he replied gallantly with a bow before turning and striding across the polished floor.

Sincerity sighed. It seemed that the room had gone suddenly dim without the elegant and magnificent Sir Simon. If only she could meet him. Sincerity frowned and returned to Miss Cobb's side.

"Cobbie, I have just had the most horrible realization."

"What is that, my dear?"

"How am I to meet anyone, to be introduced to anyone, when I have no acquaintance here in Bath?"

"Why, that is a dilemma. I mean, if your great-aunt were still alive, she would provide the entrée into society here. Your mother no doubt has a few connections, even here in Bath. . . ."

"But we dare not write to her about that!" exclaimed Sincerity.

"There, there, my dear. Do not frown so; it will only give you wrinkles. I'm certain we will think of something."

"Oh, let's go home for now. I have the headache."

"Perhaps you should try the waters," quipped Miss Cobb.

"How very droll, Cobbie," replied Sincerity.

# FOUR

Sir Simon McKendrick left the Pump Room and crossed over Stall Street to the White Hart Inn, passing the front entrance and making his way to the stables where his favorite gelding waited patiently for their daily ride.

"Angus had th' cook make up a few sandwiches, Sir Simon, just like always," said his former batman who had chosen to serve his old commanding officer in the stables instead of becoming his personal valet.

"Thank you, Patrick. How is Buttercup's leg this morning?"

"On th' mend, sir, on th' mend. She'll be ready t' go back in th' traces in a day or two."

"Thank heavens for that. Nothing worse than losing one of a matched pair," said Sir Simon, leading the gelding out of the stall and swinging up on its back with ease.

"Will you be back for th' Langs' gaming night?" asked the groom.

Simon chuckled. "Why don't you say what you mean, Patrick? What you want to know is, will I be back in time for old Soldier here to rest and have some oats before taking him out for the evening."

"Aye, that is a concern, sir."

"Yes, I'll be back in plenty of time. But I won't be

taking Soldier out tonight anyway. Miss Lang has kindly offered to send a carriage for me and Mr. Farguson."

"Ah, Miss Lang, is it?"

"Yes, Miss Lang, and you can wipe that silly grin off your face. I only agreed because I knew her late brother."

The older man laughed and said, "Of course, th' fact that she has beautiful red hair and th' face of an angel could have naught t' do with it."

"Devil take you," said Simon, raising his riding crop in salute before setting forth.

His course took him from Stall Street to Southgate Street, where he crossed the Old Bridge. He hardly spared a glance for the remains of the medieval chapel as he made his way up to Beechen Cliff, a four-hundred-foot promontory overlooking Bath.

When he had reached the top, he dismounted, hobbled his horse, and removed its bridle. Untying a bag from the saddle, he wandered to the edge of the cliff and sat down, gazing across the valley for a few minutes before opening the black satchel.

He pulled out two sandwiches of thick slabs of ham and cheese on hearty rolls and a large flask containing ale. He took a long pull on the flask and sighed. The green valley reminded him of home, of Galloway, and of his Annie's eyes. He couldn't really see her face anymore unless he took out the small miniature she'd had painted for him before he left to fight in the war. But he could still see those cool green eyes.

Simon set aside the food impatiently and pulled out his sketch pad and pastels from the bag. He returned to the sketch he had begun the day before and frowned. The shapes and colors were right, but he just couldn't capture the serenity of the scene. He ripped the page out of the book and began again, working almost feverishly, like a man driven, until the light began to fade.

Simon fought the frustration and gloom that settled

over him as the sun began to droop, but it was impossible. That familiar, quiet anger had him in its grips and refused to be shaken off. With a grunt of self-derision, he shoved his materials back in the bag along with the forgotten sandwiches and returned to his horse.

"I don't know why the devil I keep coming up here, Soldier. I don't think I'll ever be able to recapture that peace," he said, swinging up onto the broad back. "I should have just stayed home."

"A word with you, please, miss," said the butler when the two ladies returned from the Pump Room that afternoon.

Sincerity put her hand to her throbbing temple and started to follow the butler into the drawing room, bracing herself for the worst.

"Go on upstairs, Sincerity. I will deal with this," said Miss Cobb, pushing past her charge and following the servant.

"Thank you, Cobbie," said Sincerity, relieved to have this burden lifted, but feeling cowardly nonetheless.

"What is it, Crispin?" she heard Miss Cobb intone. Sincerity smiled. When Miss Cobb put on her governess role, no one could get the best of her, not even a snooty butler.

"I have received word from Mr. Cooper's clerk that he is out of town until the end of the week, at the very least. Under the circumstances, I must ask you and your charge to leave. You are here under false pretenses. It was most improper of me to have allowed you to stay here even one night. I must insist that you remove yourselves to an inn until Miss Hartford's position here has been certified by Miss Granville's solicitor."

"I appreciate your desire to do what is proper, Mr. Crispin, but I cannot believe sending a gently reared, single lady to a hotel is the right thing to do. No, we will remain here, in Miss Granville's house, until such time as the solicitor officially hands over the keys to my charge."

"I must protest . . . ," blustered the butler.

"You may protest all you wish, but there is no one to hear you. I know you will not wish to spread gossip abroad. It would do you no credit to malign your former mistress's heir. What's more, should you wish to remain in your position, Mr. Crispin, you would do well to remember to please your new mistress!"

"That very much smacks of blackmail!" exclaimed the indignant butler.

"Call it what you will. You will not sway me from my decision. Should you persist in this course, persist in distressing my sweet mistress, I will have no compunction about advising her to dispense with your services the moment she is handed the keys to the house by Mr. Cooper," declared Miss Cobb, tears springing to her eyes, she was so uncomfortable with this role of oppressor.

"Very well, Miss Cobb. I will desist. I only hope that Mr. Cooper will substantiate your young lady's claims," replied the butler, his nose elevated and most definitely out of joint.

"I have no doubt he will, Mr. Crispin. That will be all," said Miss Cobb, standing at attention until the butler had left the room. Then she reached behind her to be sure a chair was waiting and collapsed into it gratefully.

"Perhaps we can go for a short stroll this evening," whispered Sincerity when Crispin left them alone for a moment at the gleaming dining table.

"Oh, I don't think we should," breathed Miss Cobb. "I may have persuaded him to allow us to remain, but he has been giving us the most suspicious glares all day.

And though I hate to admit it, I really think we should keep a low profile until everything is official."

"Rubbish," replied Sincerity, her voice rising to normal volume. "There is no reason for us to act as if we do not belong here, because we most certainly do! And I refuse to act like a poor relation in my own house!"

"Sincerity, I . . ."

The door that led to the kitchens opened, and the haughty butler reappeared. Sam followed him with a tray containing the next course.

"Would you care for some *bœuf à la bourguignon,* miss? Hervé's wine sauce is quite extraordinary."

"Oh, yes, thank you, Crispin," said Sincerity, blinking back her surprise. "And I know Miss Cobb will be pleased. She adores the French way of cooking. Don't you, Miss Cobb?"

"Yes, I do, thank you."

The butler busied himself with serving the beef, which was accompanied by light, fluffy potatoes and tender asparagus tips topped with a rich hollandaise sauce.

"I took the liberty of bringing up a bottle of the Bordeaux wine your great-aunt was able to lay aside before the recent contretemps with France," added Crispin. "It is the perfect complement to the beef."

"Thank you, Crispin." Sincerity took a sip and nodded. "Yes, it is delicious."

When the two servants left them alone, Sincerity raised one delicate brow in question.

Miss Cobb shrugged and whispered, "I don't know why he has suddenly become civil, but I don't wish to question it either."

"I know what it was," giggled Sincerity. "You gave him that famous governess glare, and he was lost. Now he is very probably head over heels in love with you, Cobbie."

"Nonsense!" said Miss Cobb, but her cheeks were nevertheless tinged with red.

"Why, you're blushing," whispered Sincerity with a giggle. "Perhaps it is not just Mr. Crispin who is head over heels. I grant you, he is a very imposing sort of figure."

"Sincerity, I forbid you to speak to me in such a manner!" exclaimed Miss Cobb, covering her discomfiture with a quick gulp of wine that made her cough.

"My, my," murmured Sincerity, looking as if butter wouldn't melt in her mouth.

"That's quite enough, young lady," said the governess sternly, but she could not wipe the grin from her charge's lips, nor the quivering of her own.

Instead, Miss Cobb turned the tables and asked coyly, "So do tell me why you suddenly grew pale when we were in the Pump Room this afternoon, Sincerity. There were a number of handsome gentlemen. Did someone steal your heart?"

"What nonsense! You know very well I have no intention of succumbing to such an emotion. Yes, I intend to be involved in the social life Bath has to offer, but I have no intention, absolutely none, of allowing any man to affect me."

"Brave words, my dear," murmured Miss Cobb, earning herself an angry glare that had no effect whatsoever. "What if you fall in love?"

"I am beginning to believe my mother. I am not at all sure that the emotion even exists, or should exist, in a marriage. But since I have no intention of marrying, I need not bother my head with such questions," came the haughty reply.

Miss Cobb let the subject drop, but she cast her friend a worried glance from time to time. Perhaps it was because Sincerity had been with her the longest; perhaps it was because the youngest Hartford girl had always been the quietest. For whatever reason, Sincerity brought out the maternal instincts in her in a way neither of her sisters had. What she wanted more than anything was to see Sincerity happily wed, to a man she loved deeply, a man devoted to her.

As for all that nonsense about Mr. Crispin falling in love with her? Heaven forbid such a thing would come to pass! thought Miss Cobb. She certainly had no room in her life for a man!

Sincerity's night was untroubled, even by dreams of the handsome Sir Simon. She slept late the next morning, so there was no time for strolls about the town with Sam. After peeking in on her slumbering friend, she hurried downstairs for a quick breakfast and chat with Hervé before climbing back up the stairs and settling into the comfortable chair by the fire with a favorite novel. If the hero of the book had suddenly grown long, tawny hair, she did not give it a second thought. When she reached the chapter about the grand ball, Sincerity's thoughts drifted from the page to the dressing room where her gowns were stored in several wardrobes. Setting the novel aside, she rose and walked to the dressing room where she began rummaging through the wardrobes, pulling out one gown after another.

An hour later, Miss Cobb entered Sincerity's bedroom and discovered her charge knee-deep in gowns, muttering to herself as she threw them either on the bed or the floor.

"What on earth are you doing, child?"

"I am trying to decide which of these gowns will be suitable for the Assembly Rooms tomorrow night."

"Assembly Rooms? Sincerity, I thought we agreed to keep a low profile until we had met with Mr. Cooper."

"No, you agreed, and with whom? Mr. Crispin. A butler. I never agreed, and I have every intention of going to the assembly in the Upper Rooms tomorrow night. I just can't decide what would be suitable. I don't want to wear something too grand, but I certainly don't wish to offend anyone by choosing something too provincial."

"Really, Sincerity, you cannot be serious. This is not the way to go about it. What you choose to wear has nothing to say to the matter. First, we must find some way to be introduced to people. No one will even speak to us. And after the assembly? I understand they end at eleven o'clock, at which time most of the people proceed to private balls and suppers. You and I will be forced to slink home since we have no acquaintances. Be reasonable, my dear."

"I don't care what you say, Cobbie, I am going to the assembly tomorrow night. As for introductions, I shall simply have to bump into one or two people and force an introduction."

"When we have seen Mr. Cooper and your position has been solidified, then we will go. Perhaps he will even have some idea about introductions." Her words had no effect on her charge, and she begged, "Oh, Sincerity, pray do not be so forward."

"Forward? Then how else am I to meet people? Shall I ask Crispin to introduce me? Even Mr. Cooper will not be in attendance at the assembly to introduce me!"

"No, of course not. But this is not London. Allow Mr. Cooper to put the word out who you are. That's the way to handle it. After all, you are a stranger, and in a small, closed community, everyone will be wondering who you are. With a word here or there . . ."

"So I am to wait on a solicitor before showing my face in public? I think not!"

"Oh, Sincerity, please don't do anything to cause a scandal," said Miss Cobb.

"You worry too much, Cobbie. Don't forget, I plan to

make Bath my home permanently. I won't do anything outrageous, I promise you. But if it takes a twisted ankle, or a stumble, to meet a few people, then I am certainly not too proud to do so."

"I only hope we will not be put beyond the pale."

"And I only hope I will stumble upon the right people," said Sincerity with a mischievous grin.

There was a knock on the door, and Sincerity called out her permission to enter. Crispin stood on the threshold with a tall, gangly girl peeking around his shoulder.

"Pardon me, miss, but here is the maid Miss Cobb said you required. Her name is Trudy. It seems she has arrived just in time," he said, eyeing the piles of colorful gowns.

"Yes, indeed. That will be all, Crispin. Come in, Trudy. I am Miss Hartford, and this is Miss Cobb." Pointing to the pile of gowns on the floor, Sincerity added, "You can begin by taking these gowns and packing them away in the trunks in the dressing room. Then you can sort through the rest and put them in the wardrobes."

"Very good, miss," said the girl, bobbing a curtsy.

"How are you with hair?" asked Sincerity.

Trudy bobbed another curtsy and said tentatively, "I, uh, I'll try my best, miss."

"Well, that's all we can ask," said Sincerity, smiling kindly on the new servant. "Tell me, Trudy, are you any relation to Mr. Crispin?"

"Yes, miss, I'm his niece."

"So Sam is your cousin?"

The girl frowned thoughtfully before shaking her head. "No. He's on the other side of Uncle Charles, miss. My mum's sister was married to Mr. Crispin until she died."

"And when was that?"

"Oh, it's been upward of ten years now."

"I see," said Sincerity. "Then Sam is no relation to you."

"No, miss, I suppose he's not, though we come from the same small village, Monkton Farley. Why, I've known Sam since we were babes in arms," said the maid, picking up a blue gown and folding it carefully.

"Wait a minute, Trudy. I think I'll keep that one out," said Sincerity, holding out the skirt of the deep blue gown with silver embroidery around the hem and a bow of silver tulle in the back. "I've always liked this color, haven't you, Miss Cobb?"

"It looks lovely with your eyes, my dear," said her friend. "Now, about this plan of yours . . ."

"It is quite simple, really. You and I will go to the Pump Room this afternoon. Trudy, you will accompany us so as to lend us even more propriety."

"Yes, miss," said the wide-eyed maid.

"Then we will see what we can do to wrangle an introduction or two. That way, when we go to the assembly tomorrow night, we will have one or two people who can introduce us to others and so on and so forth."

Miss Cobb moaned.

"Cheer up, Cobbie. We'll soon set everything to rights, you'll see."

"I only pray you may be right," said the older woman.

"Trudy, why don't you put those things down and then go help Miss Cobb get ready for our little outing," said Sincerity, crossing the room and pulling on the bell rope. "We'll take the landau this time, Miss Cobb."

The companion emitted another groan, but she sounded resigned this time. Sincerity grinned.

The landau was pulled by two carriage horses who had seen better days—lots of them. Sincerity made a mental note to have Mr. Cooper look out for another pair as well as two suitable lady's hacks.

She knew Miss Cobb was an intrepid horsewoman,

but for herself, she would ask for a plodder. Her sister Chastity had had a huge stallion to ride, and Sincerity had admired her so, but she could not envision herself mounted on such a beast.

"We'll stop at the bookstore on the way home if you'd like, Cobbie."

"Oh, yes, that would be delightful. Did you say it was well stocked?"

"I really didn't see very much," said Sincerity, feeling the heat rise in her cheeks as she recalled her encounter with the hard-chested Sir Simon, but she related none of this to Miss Cobb. Instead, she smiled sweetly and declared, "I decided to wait until you could go with me."

"How thoughtful of you, my dear," said Miss Cobb, not believing her former pupil's whisker for a second. Whatever had caused Sincerity to avoid the bookstore, it was not consideration for her former governess.

Arriving at the Pump Room in her great-aunt's carriage proved to be a clever happenstance. As Sam helped the ladies descend, one of Great-Aunt Prudence's acquaintances was just entering the building. She turned, raised her lorgnette to her sunken eyes, and watched their progress.

"Excuse me, miss," she intoned, "but is that not the carriage of Miss Prudence Granville?"

"Yes, it is. Miss Granville was my great-aunt."

"I see," she replied, turning and taking her footman's arm to continue up the steps.

"Did you know my great-aunt, ma'am?" asked Sincerity, hurrying to catch up with the grande dame.

"Of course I did. Everyone knew her. What is your name, girl?"

"Sincerity Prudence Hartford, ma'am."

"Hartford? I don't recall any Hartfords coming to visit, though I know a Hartford. As a matter of fact, I don't recall anyone paying Prudence Granville a visit in the past ten years that I have lived here," said the old woman, once again magnifying her terrifying stare with the gold-rimmed lorgnette.

"That is because Miss Granville was a recluse who disliked every member of her family, and, I have no doubt, everyone else, too," replied Miss Cobb tartly.

The old woman began to cackle, the sound turning to a wheezing cough before she finally finished.

She turned back to Sincerity and said, "I am Lady Rutherford. You will call on me tomorrow afternoon at three o'clock, Miss Hartford. Give her a card," she barked to her servant, a mousy woman who quickly produced the card, handing it to Miss Cobb.

"Thank you, my lady," said Sincerity, dropping a quick curtsy as the older woman passed into the Pump Room.

"Whatever were you worried about?" whispered Sincerity gleefully.

Once inside the Pump Room, they ordered tea and listened to the orchestra while the rest of the visitors politely ignored their existence. Lady Rutherford, after sputtering her way through two glasses of the vile water, made her way to the door, passing them without acknowledging their presence.

Sir Simon's young people, as Sincerity had privately termed them, were once again in attendance, but Simon was not. Every time the group looked toward the door, Sincerity's gaze traveled there also, expecting and hoping, but it was not to be. Finally, deflated and weary of the scene, Sincerity and Miss Cobb left the elegant Pump Room behind.

They had the carriage drop them in Milsom Street, telling Sam that they would walk home when they had finished their shopping. With the wide-eyed Trudy in tow, Sincerity and Miss Cobb entered the modiste's establishment and were greeted by an eager clerk.

"Only look at this lovely watered silk, Miss Cobb."

"I don't think that would suit your coloring, Sincerity," said Miss Cobb, making a face at the dull green color.

"Not for me, you goose. For you, of course."

"For me? I have all the gowns I need, my dear."

"Perhaps, but one can always use a new gown. Why don't you have your measurements taken, and then we can decide on a style."

"Right this way, ladies," said the clerk, leading them to a back room.

When they were left alone for a moment, Cobbie whispered, "Sincerity, I thought we were going to wait until we saw Mr. Cooper."

"Well, it never hurts to be ready. Besides, the bill won't be sent 'round for weeks," replied her charge.

"Oh," groaned Miss Cobb. "I knew you couldn't be patient."

"Sh! Here she comes. Now you just let me treat you to this gown. I insist!"

When they left the dressmaker's shop, Sincerity pulled Miss Cobb into the milliner's, losing no time in purchasing the blue bonnet she had seen in the window on her first visit.

"Sincerity, we should go home. It's getting late."

"It's not that late, and we haven't even gone to the bookseller's yet."

"Very well. I know we can't get into too much trouble there," said Miss Cobb, unaware of the extent of her inability to look into the future.

They entered the shop without Sincerity running into another broad-chested gentleman, and began to browse through the latest novels. Miss Cobb, who believed novels were fine, but that the mind should not be neglected, left Sincerity's side and wandered away. While she was deciding between two volumes of French poems, one by

Villon and the other by Ronsard, Sincerity approached the clerk to make her purchases.

"Two novels," commented the older man with a smile.

"Yes, you know how we ladies like novels," said Sincerity with her best smile. "The gentlemen, I believe, choose more serious works."

"Usually, but there are a few who prefer novels."

"Oh, like Sir Simon?"

"Oh yes, Sir Simon," said the clerk, handing back her change.

"Perhaps he is buying them for his wife," prodded Sincerity.

"I don't think so. I understand, from the conversation of our customers, of course, that he is a widower."

"Oh, yes, how silly of me to forget," she replied with a trill of laughter that suggested she had not two thoughts to rub together.

"Sincerity, are you ready?" asked Miss Cobb, handing both volumes to the clerk with a cold stare that made the clerk fumble nervously with the till.

"Yes. I was just waiting for you, Miss Cobb."

"Will there be anything else, madam?" stammered the clerk.

"No, thank you. That will be all," she replied, paying for her purchase and pulling Sincerity out the door.

"What on earth were you thinking, making such personal comments about a stranger! And right out in public where anyone might hear you! And who, pray tell, is this Sir Simon? And where did you meet him?" demanded Miss Cobb in urgent whispers as they strolled casually up Milsom Street.

"Cobbie, do calm down, or you will do yourself a mischief. I was only making conversation. I have never even met this Sir Simon. What is more, no one overheard me, and I promise not to speak of him again. There! Now are you satisfied?" Sincerity tossed her head, sending the curls that clustered around her face bobbing back and forth.

"You have never met him?" asked Miss Cobb suspiciously. She knew her charge's tendency to stretch the truth in order to extricate herself from a difficult situation, and she watched her response with narrowed gaze.

But Sincerity looked her in the eye and declared, "Certainly not! How could I have done so? Since we arrived in Bath, I haven't been introduced to anyone except Lady Rutherford, and you were present for that!" This was true, she rationalized; she had run into the handsome Sir Simon, not been introduced. But she turned the subject adroitly, adding, "Now, please, let us go home. I find I am positively famished!"

"Very well. I'm sorry to be so short-tempered, my dear. I suppose it is the strain of our situation. Please forgive me."

"Of course, dearest Cobbie," said Sincerity with her sweetest smile.

They were soon home again, an appellation that Sincerity enjoyed flaunting every chance she had.

"Home," she said with a voluble sigh, sinking onto the sofa in the drawing room.

"Yes, home," echoed Miss Cobb, taking the chair next to the sofa. In a low voice, she added, "I hope we are still saying that after Mr. Cooper's visit on Friday."

"What? Of course we shall!" said Sincerity.

Mr. Crispin entered the room, clearing his throat to gain their attention.

"Yes?"

"The Master of Ceremonies has called, Miss Hartford. Are you at home?"

"Oh, yes, please," said Sincerity, sitting up straighter and winking at Miss Cobb. Crispin returned a moment later and announced their visitor. "How do you do, sir?

I am Miss Hartford, formerly of Folkestone. This is my companion, Miss Cobb."

He was an older man, but he made a creditable leg, declining the chair Miss Cobb offered him. "In my official capacity, I wanted to welcome you both to Bath, Miss Hartford and Miss Cobb."

"How very kind of you," said Sincerity, greatly enjoying her role as the lady of the house.

"Not at all. You are no doubt planning to attend the assemblies?" he asked, his single gray eyebrow rising as he phrased the question.

"Indeed, we are looking forward to it," said Sincerity.

"Wonderful, wonderful. Now, there is the matter of the subscription fee, ladies. I can . . ."

"Subscription fee?" asked Sincerity. She hadn't thought about that particular stumbling block. She and Miss Cobb had almost exhausted their small funds. There was no way she could give this man the money he required. How lowering! It would be all over Bath that Miss Sincerity Hartford was a nothing, a nobody, until her great-aunt had bequeathed a tidy fortune on her. And just how tidy of a fortune was it? she wondered for the hundredth time.

"I'm afraid we don't keep very many funds in the house, sir," said Miss Cobb smoothly.

"No, no, you misunderstand me, Miss Cobb. Miss Hartford, you may tell your man of affairs about the fee so that he can attend to it. If that will be convenient?" he added.

"Why, of course it is. Thank you for thinking of that, Mr. Grant. I'm afraid I have no head where money is concerned," said Sincerity with a coy trill of laughter.

"Ah, you ladies . . . ," he said, wagging a large finger at her. "If there is anything I can do to make your stay more comfortable, please let me know, ladies. Until the assembly tomorrow night, then. Good day."

When he had gone, Miss Cobb mopped her brow with her handkerchief and observed, "That was a very near thing."

"Near, but neatly avoided. As I have told you before, Cobbie, this is where we were meant to be!"

# FIVE

Sincerity Hartford was content to spend the evening sitting over her embroidery, toiling away on the small tapestry that was one day destined to cover a footstool. The fact that she took few stitches during the course of the evening was not lost on her mentor, but Miss Cobb, happily reading from her new book of French verse, was wise enough not to inquire into what was occupying her charge's thoughts. They sat in the comfortable drawing room in companionable silence.

Yawning, Sincerity finally set aside her needle and canvas, rising and stretching her stiff muscles with a groan. "I think I will go to bed early tonight, Cobbie. We have a busy day tomorrow, what with the visit to Lady Rutherford and the assembly in the Upper Rooms."

"Very true," said Miss Cobb. "I think I'll just read a little longer. Good night, my dear."

"Good night."

Sincerity climbed the stairs to her room two at a time, her energy at odds with the large yawn she had evinced moments before. She had not admitted to Cobbie what was really on her mind. Sleep was the farthest thing from it. Trudy helped her dress for bed, and Sincerity climbed in and blew out the candle, smiling in the dark and hugging to herself her fantasies.

Since childhood, she had escaped reality by weaving

daydreams. It was her way of blocking out her mother's and twin sister's demands. To be fair, Tranquility hadn't forced Sincerity to join in her escapades; she had merely expected it. So through years of practice, Sincerity learned to follow wherever her twin led while her mind would take her to the places she only read about in storybooks.

Sometimes Sincerity thought she had been happiest in her dreamworlds. They were stories of dragons and knights, damsels and sorcerers. Grown-up now, her daydreams were the stuff of the novels she read, with dashing heroes who fell in love with her and worshiped at her feet.

Usually, she could weave her daydreams during any quiet moment, but something about the one she was spinning since arriving in Bath prevented her from keeping silent. Downstairs, sitting in the drawing room with Cobbie, she had been unable to escape completely into her new story where the hero was tall and broad-chested, with fine calves showing beneath the plaid kilt he wore, and tawny gold hair blowing free in the wind. Alone in her bed, she arrived at the part where he declared his undying love for her, and her sigh of happiness was audible.

Smiling, she fell asleep.

In the drawing room, Cobbie's book of poetry slipped from her hands, resting on her bony chest. Her eyes closed and her breath came in even waves.

She awoke suddenly, startled.

"Oh, Miss Cobb, I beg your pardon," said Crispin, holding his candle up high.

Miss Cobb rubbed her eyes and smiled. "Quite all right, Mr. Crispin. I must have fallen asleep over my poetry. I suppose Ronsard is not as captivating as I had imagined he would be."

*"Et des amours desquelles nous parlons,*

*Quand serons morts, ne sera plus nouvelle!*
*Pource aimez-moi, cependant qu'êtes belle."*

"You know Ronsard?" demanded the unflappable Miss Cobb, looking at the formal butler with new respect.

"I enjoy his work, yes," replied the butler, his inflexible features softened by the candlelight that turned his gray hair to silver.

"And your French is very good," she added, her surprise causing her to forget her manners and their roles.

"Mrs. Granville traveled extensively whenever the political situation in Europe allowed. Do you require anything else, ma'am? Fresh candles, perhaps?" offered the butler, straightening his back and resuming his proper role.

"No, thank you. I think I will retire," she said, rising and moving toward the door. "Good night, Mr. Crispin."

"Good night, Miss Cobb."

Miss Cobb climbed the stairs to her room. Trudy was waiting to help her change for bed. When she was under the counterpane, she picked up the volume of poetry and searched for the passage Crispin had quoted. She discovered it in the fifth sonnet about Cassandre, a young lady the poet had loved in his youth.

Translating as she read, Miss Cobb murmured softly, "And the loves we have spoken of, when we are dead, will no longer be new. Therefore, love me, while you are still beautiful." She smiled, closing her eyes and remembering the tone of his voice.

Suddenly, she put the book on the nightstand and blew out the candles before impatiently jerking the counterpane into place under her chin.

"What nonsense!" she said forcefully to the darkened room.

The next afternoon Sincerity and Miss Cobb ordered out the carriage for the short ride to the Royal Crescent where Lady Rutherford resided. Sincerity wore a pale green carriage dress and a fetching bonnet with matching ribbons tied under her chin. Her kid gloves, dyed green also, were short, just covering her wrists. Miss Cobb was resplendent in an elegant lavender silk gown that was beautifully cut, without the distraction of lace and ruffles. Her bonnet was straw, dyed a pale gray, with lavender silk roses.

Sincerity found she was quite looking forward to the visit. By careful questioning of Hervé, who was friends and sometimes rivals with her ladyship's cook, she had discovered that Lady Rutherford was another matron who lived alone. Granted, Lady Rutherford, like her great-aunt, was elderly. But, Sincerity reasoned, why couldn't she live quietly and independently in Bath, since she now had the means.

On this happy thought, the carriage pulled up in front of the imposing structure that was the Royal Crescent, designed in the previous century by the famous architect, John Wood the younger. Sincerity's mouth rounded in awe at the sight of the thirty terraced houses, separated by massive Ionic columns, built in a perfect crescent shape.

"How lovely," said Miss Cobb, climbing down and dragging her charge up the steps to the front door.

Sincerity handed her calling card to the butler and waited to be announced.

"This is much more magnificent than Great-Aunt Prudence's house," she whispered.

"Yes, but no more comfortable, I am sure," responded Miss Cobb loyally.

"This way, ladies. Her ladyship will see you now," said the butler, leading them into the formal drawing room where Lady Rutherford sat in a high-backed chair, an ugly pug dog sleeping in her lap.

"Good afternoon, my lady," said Sincerity, dropping a curtsy before her hostess.

"Humph! Well, come in, come in. Have a seat. You too, Miss Cobb, is it?"

"Yes, my lady," replied Miss Cobb taking the seat farthest from the crabby old woman.

"Not there. Come over here where I can talk to you. And you, Miss Hartford, this is my granddaughter, Lizzie," she said, motioning a young girl forward. "You girls go sit by the window and tell me if anyone worth noticing comes along."

Sincerity shot a perplexed look at Miss Cobb before she pasted on a smile and did as she was bid. While listening to the seventeen-year-old Lizzie, she kept one ear alert to be certain Lady Rutherford wasn't running roughshod over Miss Cobb.

"Are you to go to the assembly tonight, Miss Hartford?" asked the pretty young lady.

"Yes, though I do not have many acquaintances here in Bath. I shall probably be forced to sit and watch the dancing."

"Poppycock! I'll see to it you meet the gentlemen, and Lizzie knows a few of the young ladies," cackled Lady Rutherford, from across the room, easily inserting herself into their conversation before returning to her own.

Lizzie giggled and leaned closer to her guest, saying, "Please do not heed my grandmother's forceful manner, Miss Hartford. She has always said whatever she pleased to anyone she wanted. But in this case, I think she means well, and I for one will be glad if you will stand by my side. Perhaps then the gentlemen won't be so afraid to come up and ask for a dance."

"The gentlemen don't ask you for dances, Lizzie? I find that hard to credit, someone as pretty as you."

Lizzie Montfort blushed a rosy pink and shook her

head, lowering her voice even more, so that Sincerity had to move closer.

"Some of the gentlemen will, of course, but they are usually very, uh, energetic. I find myself overwhelmed by them. I would like to meet someone more like myself, someone quiet and reserved. Then I wouldn't mind the assemblies so." She winced and ducked her head, glancing in the direction of her grandmother, who, fortunately, was too engrossed in conversation with Miss Cobb to have overheard her granddaughter's comments.

"Will you be going to London for the Season next year?" asked Sincerity, strangely drawn to this younger girl. After all, she had grown up being the one who was quiet, the follower. It was gratifying to be able to offer comfort and a sympathetic ear to someone even more timid than she was.

"Yes," said the girl, shuddering delicately. "If I do not become betrothed this year in Bath, my parents are going to send me to my aunt in London."

"I take it you do not like the idea," said Sincerity.

"No, I mean, I know it is wonderful to have the opportunity, but . . . I am afraid my aunt would choose someone totally unsuited to my temperament. She has always cared deeply about social positions and such."

"My mother is much the same. What is your aunt's name?"

"Lady Humphries," replied Lizzie. "Do you know her?"

"A little. She and my mother are friends. They both think the same way, but you were saying you don't agree?"

"Not really. Papa is a scholar. He runs a small school for boys. I was taught that there are more important things than titles and such. That is, I don't wish to sound ungrateful, but . . ."

"But you would rather meet someone this summer in

Bath and be married," said Sincerity with a smile. "Don't worry. I shan't tell anyone your secret."

"You are most kind, Miss Hartford."

"Now, you must call me Sincerity if I am to call you Lizzie."

"Very well, thank you. That is a most unusual name," she added, then turned scarlet and stammered, "It is very pretty, of course."

Sincerity laughed. "Don't worry. I am not so easily offended. These names run in our family, I'm afraid. My mother's name is Divinity, and she carried on the absurd notion by giving all of her daughters similar names. My twin sister is Tranquility, and my other sister is Chastity."

"How delightful!"

"You would not think so if you had to live with such a name," commented Sincerity.

"But with your name, you are out of the common way, don't you think? And you would never want for a topic of conversation in social exchanges. Your name alone . . ."

"Come over here, Lizzie, and pour out for us. You need to practice. And see that you're careful with the cups this time," said her grandmother. "She's broken one already this visit."

Lizzie turned pink, and her hands began to shake. Sincerity quickly took the cup and saucer from her new friend's hands and handed it to Lady Rutherford. Lizzie flashed her a look of undying gratitude, and Sincerity winked at her.

They spoke of the weather and the coming assembly for the next fifteen minutes. Then Miss Cobb rose, signaling the end of their visit.

"Humph!" breathed Sincerity when the door had closed behind them. "Lady Rutherford is a regular tartar. I feel sorry for Lizzie."

"Hm, I wonder," said Miss Cobb, her brow crinkling in concern.

"Wonder about what? Whatever did you manage to talk about before tea? I'm sorry I abandoned you, but I had my orders," said Sincerity with a grin.

"That was fine. Actually, she did most of the talking. She must have asked me a hundred questions about your great-aunt. I think she called you two back over because she realized I had no information to impart. I'm just puzzled by her interest."

"They were friends, weren't they?"

"Oh, I didn't get that impression. Perhaps rivals would be the better term. Oh, well, it needn't concern us. What matters is that she has agreed to sponsor you, of sorts. She mentioned that her daughter knows your mother. But you should have a full dance card tonight! Won't that be a treat!"

"I can hardly wait," said Sincerity dryly.

For the assembly, Sincerity chose a full-skirted gown of rose-colored silk, one of her favorites. She had worn it so often in London, her mother had ordered it thrown away, but she had saved it from the charity bag. The fabric moved deliciously with every step, and she looked forward to the admiring glances she was sure to garner at the assembly. Trudy arranged her blond hair in springy curls around her face, twisting the longer locks into a knot on the crown of her head. Standing back, the abigail declared earnestly that her mistress looked like an angel. Sincerity thanked her for the compliment, and then they descended on Miss Cobb to help her along in her toilette.

Miss Cobb wore a becoming gown of pearl gray and had pulled her graying brown hair into a tight chignon at the nape of her neck. She had inserted two silver silk rosebuds into the bun, but the effect was not pleasing.

"No, no, Cobbie, you must allow Trudy to do your hair tonight if we mean to make a splash," said Sincerity, dragging her former governess back to the dressing table and sitting her down on the bench in front of the mirror.

"Really, Sincerity, I have no desire to make a splash, as you term it. I am quite comfortable with my appearance as it is," she said, starting to rise.

Sincerity pulled the roses from the bun and then began removing the pins.

"Leave it alone," protested Miss Cobb. "Now look what you've done. I'll have to start all over."

"Let Trudy do it," said Sincerity.

"Please, Miss Cobb. You've got beautiful long hair. It will be such a treat t' work with it," said the maid, winking at Sincerity over the head of the older woman.

"Well, if you don't mind. Only don't make it all curly like Sincerity's. That's all well and good for youthful ladies, but for someone my age, I find it inappropriate."

"Don't you worry, Miss Cobb. Just sit still, and let's see what I can do."

The woman who stared at her reflection some ten minutes later was speechless. She rose and turned, smiled and twisted back to the mirror to be certain she hadn't been mistaken in the image.

"Well, what do you think, Cobbie?" demanded Sincerity, clapping her hands together gleefully.

"Do you like it, Miss Cobb?" asked the maid anxiously. "Because if you don't, you've only t' say th' word, and I'll . . ."

"No, no, I like it very well. I vow, Trudy, your talent is amazing. How you can take this mass of hair and with a few twists and turns, make it absolutely elegant . . . Well, it's a mystery to me, my girl! But you have real talent in those hands, I want you to know."

"Thank you, Miss Cobb. I'm so glad you like it!"

"You know, Cobbie, I may not be the only one with a full dance card tonight," quipped Sincerity.

"Now you are being excessive, young lady," said Miss

Cobb, but she smiled, pleased. "Thank you again, Trudy. Come along, Sincerity. We don't want to be too late."

Miss Cobb and Sincerity made their way downstairs where Mr. Crispin waited, opening the door for them with a flourish. He might pretend to have reservations about Sincerity's claim to her late aunt's house and property, but he could not hide the admiration in his eyes when he gazed on his new mistress and the graceful Miss Cobb.

"We shan't be too late, Crispin," said Sincerity, grinning when he couldn't drag his eyes away from Miss Cobb.

"Very good, miss," he said, nodding to her. Then his gaze returned to Miss Cobb, and he bowed, adding, "Enjoy yourselves, ladies."

Miss Cobb managed a cool smile, but she didn't speak.

Sincerity's giggle finally escaped when Sam had closed the carriage door, but she was stared into silence by Miss Cobb's raised chin and pursed lips. She could not silence her thoughts and began to weave a new tale in her mind, this one ending with Cobbie and Crispin living happily ever after.

"Here we are, ladies. I told Clarence we'd be waiting in the side street for you, just in case you should want to leave early."

"Really, I don't think that is necessary," said Sincerity.

"Nevertheless, Sam, we appreciate it," interrupted Miss Cobb, taking her charge's arm and heading toward the bright lights of the Upper Assembly rooms.

"Why did you tell him that?" whispered Sincerity. "Do you think something is going to go wrong?"

"Of course not, but it never hurts to have an escape planned, just in case. If you don't, I've always felt it is rather like thumbing one's nose at the fates."

Sincerity frowned. Miss Cobb was acting so strangely.

Perhaps she really was falling love with Crispin, thought Sincerity.

"The exterior certainly doesn't do the interior justice," whispered Miss Cobb as they waited to be announced.

"It certainly doesn't. I vow, it is more elegant than Almack's," returned Sincerity.

"Never let anyone in London hear you say that, miss," said a young man behind her. Sincerity turned to find two merry brown eyes gazing at her, rather like a hopeful puppy. With another smile, he confessed, "I'm so sorry. It's a frightful habit of mine, eavesdropping."

"A shocking habit," intoned Miss Cobb. "Come along, Sincerity."

"Good-bye," she managed to say before being propelled into the ballroom.

Sincerity quickly forgot about the impertinent gentleman as she gazed about her at the sparkling white walls with gold trim and the massive chandeliers that hung from the ceiling, each one gleaming with the light of countless candles.

"Much prettier than Almack's," she said again.

"There is Lady Rutherford. I suppose we should join her. We don't wish to run the risk of being accosted by any more brazen young men," said Miss Cobb.

"I don't know, Cobbie. Sometimes it is delightful being accosted by brazen young men."

"Tran . . . Sincerity, do watch your tongue! I almost called you Tranquility just then; she was ever one to forget her manners!"

"Cobbie, I am not a green girl. I do not need you to tell me what to say or not to say. My comment was for your ears only. There is no need to take on so."

"Oh, yes, my dear. You're quite right. I suppose it is just the thought of spending the evening conversing with—or rather listening to—Lady Rutherford."

"Well, why don't you dance? I'm sure there is nothing to prevent you from taking to the floor."

"Surely you jest, Sincerity. I am a spinster of thirty-eight years; dancing is not for me. Besides, I am hardly of the same station . . ."

"I wager your station as the granddaughter of a baronet puts you above half the people in attendance. But that is neither here nor there, my dearest Cobbie. Now that we are in Bath, we are equal. Whatever I have is yours," said Sincerity, taking her friend's hand and giving it a quick squeeze.

"Why, Sincerity, I . . . I don't know what to say," said Miss Cobb, tears springing to her eyes.

"Then you needn't say anything. As for Lady Rutherford, we will not cut the connection, of course. After all, I understand she is a force to be reckoned with in Bath. But we don't have to sit in her pocket after this evening. Remember, we have only ourselves to please!" said Sincerity, stepping forward and curtsying to Lizzie's crabby grandmother with a smile.

"Good evening, my lady," she said. "I trust you are well this evening?"

"Humph! Well enough. Run along and talk to Lizzie. She's talking to that young man about pigs. Don't know why the girl can't keep to the weather. Come closer, Miss Cobb, and have a seat. Only look at that silly female over there in the huge turban. Have you ever seen anything so ugly?"

Miss Cobb did as she was bid, but she did not respond to Lady Rutherford's comment. It wasn't necessary since the old woman didn't even pause in her caustic observations, progressing around the room and shredding the fashion sense of every female, and some of the males, in sight.

Sincerity and Lizzie greeted each other warmly, and she introduced Sincerity to the gentleman beside her.

"How do you do, Miss Hartford?"

"How do you do, Mr. Nelson? Are you perhaps related to our naval hero, Admiral Nelson?" she inquired politely.

Mr. Nelson was an older man, much too old for little Lizzie, thought Sincerity. Lizzie was probably quite comfortable in his company since he wasn't trying to empty the butter boat over her head with compliments. But he was much too dull for the sweet-tempered girl she had met earlier in the day.

"No, no, I have no such claim to fame. My family is from Yorkshire, always has been. We raise pigs."

"Oh, uh, how fascinating that must be. Do you reside in Bath or are you merely visiting?"

"I am visiting. I brought my mother on the advice of her physician. Unfortunately, she is not well enough to join us this evening, but I was telling Miss Montfort all about her."

"Indeed, I understood Lady Rutherford to say that you were discussing pigs," said Sincerity, stifling a giggle.

But the man was too obtuse to catch her cutting comment, merely imparting thoughtfully, "No, we were speaking about the pigs earlier. They are fascinating animals, though most people don't know that. I have one boar that you would swear is human. He's a . . ."

"But you were telling me about your mother, Mr. Nelson," said Lizzie, obviously appalled to be returning to the previous topic.

"What? Yes, yes. When you arrived, Miss Hartford, I was just about to tell Miss Montfort what the physician said about my mother's boils. . . ."

"Really! Well, I hate to interrupt, but I must confess, Mr. Nelson, that if I don't have some sort of refreshment soon, I am likely to faint. I don't suppose I could . . . impose. . . ." Sincerity waited for him to take the hint. When his perception failed him once again, she said bluntly, "Please go and fetch us something cool to drink, Mr. Nelson. Thank you so much."

"Well, yes, of course. Happy to oblige, Miss Hartford. I know what it is to be thirsty. You have no idea what it is to be thirsty if you haven't been out in a pigsty all day in the summer. Now that's thirsty. You can't get . . ."

"Mr. Nelson?" interrupted Sincerity with a simper. "Our drinks?"

"What? Oh, yes, yes. Right away," he said, turning and toddling away.

"How in the world did you manage that?" asked Lizzie, her eyes wide with admiration for her new friend.

"That? It's nothing. In no time, you'll learn how to handle an awkward situation like that. I admire your patience. I believe I would have perished from boredom long ago," laughed Sincerity.

"But he didn't even guess that you were trying to get rid of him. However did you manage that?"

"Never mind for now. We must be elsewhere when he returns." Sincerity walked over to Lady Rutherford and spoke quietly for a moment before turning and motioning Lizzie forward.

"Come with me," she instructed.

"Where are we going?"

"To the ladies withdrawing room. You have torn your shawl, and I am going to mend it for you," she said quietly, enjoying the novel experience of being the leader for the first time in her life.

"But I haven't . . . Oh, I see," said the girl with a giggle.

Even after Tranquility had wed and gone off to France, Sincerity had been unable to shake her reputation as a follower, almost a cipher. It was not that she had tried so very hard to shake her old image. It was much more comfortable being the one everyone imposed on, the one who was always handy to fill out a set in a country dance or even up the numbers at the dinner table.

They spent several minutes pretending to repair the nonexistent tear in Lizzie's shawl, all for the benefit of the maids and the other ladies who happened to enter the room. Finally, Sincerity led the way back to the ballroom, pausing at the edge of the hall and surveying the assembly.

"Now, we mustn't hurry, Lizzie, or Mr. Nelson will still be waiting on us, and I vow I will scream if I have to listen to his conversation for another second."

"He was so very dreadful," agreed Lizzie. "I just didn't know what to do about it."

"Never mind. I'll teach you how to depress the attentions of gentlemen like that. I really don't understand how they can believe their conversation is so enthralling," said Sincerity with a worldly laugh for her pupil.

She continued with calculating iciness, "Now, after a few minutes, we'll return to your grandmother, but by a circular route, so that we don't run the risk of meeting up with the mind-numbing Mr. Nelson."

"How clever of you, Sincerity," came the gratifying response.

"Trying to shake a particularly annoying suitor, are you? Poor devil," said a low voice, so close to Sincerity's ear that she jumped.

"Why, you startled me, sir," she said, whirling around to face the eavesdropper from earlier in the evening.

"I fear I often have that effect on the ladies, much to my sorrow," he quipped mournfully. Lizzie giggled, and he leaned toward her. "Perhaps one of you charming ladies will take pity on a poor ex-soldier."

"But we have not been introduced," said Lizzie, lowering her lashes and looking at the floor while her color changed to a charming pink.

"Leave the young ladies alone, Jackson," said another

masculine voice, his authoritative tone causing the young man to straighten obediently.

Sincerity's heart jumped to her throat. There could be no mistaking the slight Scottish inflection or the delightful tremor his voice sent tripping up her spine. She spun around. Unfortunately, her dancing shoes slipped on the polished marble, and she lost her balance, careening out of control until strong hands righted her again, setting her firmly on her feet. He disengaged himself immediately.

"Oh, thank you, sir," she breathed, wishing the floor could open up and swallow her whole.

Sir Simon released her and said stiffly, "You're welcome, miss." Then he looked over her head at his friend and drawled, "If you want an introduction, Jackson, you'll have to do things properly, as I am sure this sophisticated and worldly young woman here would tell you, if she had been introduced to you, which she has not."

"You surely know how to spoil a fellow's fun, Simon," said Jackson before turning back to Lizzie and lifting her hand to his lips for a chaste salute. "Very well, I will leave. But I give you fair warning, fair maiden; I shall not rest until I have you in my arms . . . for a waltz."

When the two had departed, Lizzie expelled a little squeal of excitement. "Have you ever heard anything so wonderful? How elegant and refined he is."

"Yes, he is that," murmured Sincerity. She could feel the heat of embarrassment in her cheeks. Sir Simon had heard her arrogant comments and pronounced judgment accordingly. She had seen the derision in his eyes. He must think her a vain female! Oh, how could she have had the ill fortune to be overheard by the handsome Sir Simon?

And handsome he was, dressed in his evening clothes.

His snowy cravat was tied to perfection and his shirt points, though fashionable, were not so high that he had trouble turning his head. No, there was nothing of the dandy in his dress. She had seen Beau Brummel on several occasions. To her mind, Sir Simon was twice as elegant as the Beau, and ten times as handsome.

No doubt he was repelled by her mean, ruthless comment. Not that she had any hopes in that direction. Certainly not, she assured herself. Now that she had her inheritance, the last thing she wanted was to become entangled with a man! All the same, it was lowering to think she had given him such a shocking opinion of her.

Lizzie sighed again, saying dreamily, "Jackson, isn't that a lovely name?" She paused for her mentor to make a comment. When none was forthcoming, she asked, "Shall we go back to my grandmother now? I don't see Mr. Nelson anywhere."

"What? Yes, yes, of course," managed Sincerity, frowning at her new friend. How on earth could the silly chit be mooning over that boy when Sir Simon was obviously the better man?

They slowly made their way around the ballroom, and all the while, Sincerity continued to berate herself for her gauche observations. It wasn't at all like her to voice her outrageous opinions. Her mother had always warned her to keep her thoughts to herself . . . which was why, no doubt, so many offers were made for her hand. The gentlemen all thought she would make a biddable wife. Little did they know—or care, for that matter—what she thought.

"Sincerity, is something the matter? Have I said anything to offend you? I mean, if you wish to dance with Mr. Jackson, I will certainly step aside. He was probably just talking to me because he was so in awe of you."

Sincerity stopped their progress and shook her head, smiling once again. "Now that is a great deal of folderol, Lizzie. It was obvious Mr. Jackson was smitten with you from the moment he set eyes on you. And I am sorry to be so quiet. I assure you I have no designs on Mr. Jackson."

"Oh, good. I mean, I am glad . . . That is . . ."

"I know what you mean," said Sincerity, managing another smile for her apprentice and linking arms with her.

"Come along, Simon. Let us find someone who knows the identity of that beautiful girl so I can beg an introduction," said Mr. Jackson, lately of the 92nd Highlanders. He paused midstride when he realized his old commanding officer had not stirred a step. "What are you waiting for? I saw the look you gave the pretty blonde one. Well, you can have her, as far as I'm concerned. I'm interested in the other one, the one with the doelike eyes."

"You don't know what the devil you are talking about, Peter," said Sir Simon, looking bored.

"The devil I don't," said his younger friend. "She fairly bowled you over; I could tell."

"The deuce you say. No, I just thought I had met her before, but I was mistaken," lied Sir Simon, who well remembered the round lines of the beautiful girl who had sent his books flying when she careened into his chest. But he was not going to admit as much to his friend. Jackson would have every man present wagering on the nuptials if he so much as mentioned remembering the girl.

"Well, if you say so, but do come with me. Between the two of us, we should be able to find someone with a mutual acquaintance. What was the blonde's name?"

"Sincerity," replied Simon, meeting his friend's teasing eyes without blinking. "You run along, Jackson. Ask your brother for help. He knows practically everyone, the gentlemen and the ladies. I'm going to dance with Miss Lang."

"Suit yourself, Simon. But between the two, Miss Lang and this Sincerity, I think there is no comparison," said his friend.

"So much the better. Then I shall have Miss Lang all to myself," said Simon. He watched as Peter Jackson searched out his brother and pulled him to one side, cocking his head in the direction of the pretty brunette and stunning blonde.

And she was stunning, he admitted to himself. She was nothing like any of the females who had caught his eye before. Certainly, she was nothing like his Annie, who had been willowy and dark-haired. He shifted restlessly on his feet and wished he had a drink.

"Damn," he muttered quietly. He'd met the girl twice now, and she was already driving him to drink.

It wasn't just her looks that made her unforgettable. It was the uncanny way she had of entangling him, both physically, like at the booksellers, and emotionally. And she was precisely the sort of fashion-mad female that had caused him to choose Bath over London. His one Season in London as a young man had sent him running from the clutches of grasping females, back home to where the girls were honest and charming. For all he knew, this Sincerity had planned to run into him at the booksellers. He had heard all about London ladies who would stop at nothing to entrap a man!

He vowed to keep as far away as possible from the annoying and troublesome Sincerity. After all, he had come to Bath to cure his restlessness, not add to it.


Sincerity and Lizzie returned to Lady Rutherford's sphere and were introduced to two gentlemen who requested the next country dances. Though Sincerity conversed politely with her partner and went through the steps, her mind was busy. Soon the music stopped, and they made their way back to Lady Rutherford and Miss Cobb.

Sincerity pasted a smile on her face as Lizzie chattered on, but she was preoccupied, her mind still busy rearranging facts to suit her dreamworld. She reminded herself that Sir Simon was hardly likely to have anything else to do with her, but that it made no difference. Actually, she told herself, it was better that way. If she became well acquainted in him, she would doubtless discover the chinks in his armor, and then he would be unsuitable for her daydreams. Yes, all in all, it was best that he had developed a distaste for her early on.

"Lizzie, Miss Hartford, here are two more gentlemen come to beg an introduction," said Lady Rutherford, cackling like a hen.

Sincerity looked up to find Mr. Jackson smiling at Lizzie. Her heart leaped, but then fell when she realized the second gentleman was not Sir Simon, but another young man who bore a marked resemblance to Mr. Jackson.

"And this is Mr. Jackson's brother, Mr. David Jackson," her ladyship was saying.

"Ladies," said the duo, bowing before them.

"We are delighted to make your acquaintance," said Mr. Jackson with a grin for Lizzie.

"Quite delighted," remarked his brother.

Sincerity tugged her polite smile firmly into place. In the distance, she noticed Sir Simon leading the red-haired beauty from the Pump Room onto the ballroom floor. Her smile was a little brittle as she accepted David Jackson's invitation to join the set just forming.

So much for changing daydreams into dreams come true.

# SIX

Sincerity was returned to Miss Cobb and Lady Rutherford after the country dance. Several other gentlemen were waiting to request a dance of her and Lizzie. Sincerity smiled brightly and accepted the first one to speak, forgetting his name instantly.

When the figures of the dance brought them together, the gentleman cleared his throat loudly, and Sincerity finally noticed his face. He was older, perhaps forty years of age, with an open, pleasant face. The quality of his evening clothes bespoke his wealth, but his uneasiness in them told a different tale. Sincerity smiled at him, and the relief on his face made her giggle. The smile widened.

"There, that's better," she said, "Mr., uh . . ."

"Boynton," he supplied.

"I apologize for not remembering, Mr. Boynton. I am terrible with names."

"Think nothing of it, Miss Hartford," he replied. "I was only pleased—and surprised, I might add—when you chose me over all those good-looking young gentlemen."

"Whyever shouldn't I? You are a fine-looking gentleman, yourself."

The steps of the dance required that they change partners, so further conversation was arrested for the moment.

When they came together again, Mr. Boynton continued as if they had never parted. "Well, I thank you for the compliment, Miss Hartford, but perhaps you will want to take it back when I tell you why I really asked to dance with you."

Sincerity's expression of alarm warned Mr. Boynton that he had committed a faux pas, and he turned red, stammering, "That is, I meant no disrespect, it is just . . ."

Sincerity was thankful when the steps of the dance once again interrupted their conversation. They had only just met. She could not imagine what the large gentleman wanted to say to her, but she felt certain it would make her uncomfortable. She would have to put him in his place.

When they came together again for the finish, Sincerity leveled Mr. Boynton with a cold stare. Still, as he escorted her back to Miss Cobb's side, he tried again to explain himself. When she pretended to be deaf, he stopped and pulled her to the side of the room.

Sincerity contemplated wrenching her arm away from him, but he relinquished his hold and entreated, "I should have told you from the first; I requested a dance of you because of your companion."

Sincerity frowned, her attention caught. "Miss Cobb?"

"Yes, Miss Cobb. I asked her for a dance, but she told me she was here tonight so that you might dance, and not the other way around, so she refused."

"I am sure Miss Cobb may dance if she wishes to do so," said Sincerity.

"But when I asked her, she said she could not dance and watch over you at the same time."

"It seems you and Miss Cobb had quite a conversation, Mr. Boynton. She is not usually so talkative with strangers."

"True, but it didn't do any good. Oh, I know you

young ladies are here for the dancing, but Miss Cobb is not so old, and she is certainly closer to my age."

"You speak as if you are well acquainted with her, sir."

"And so I am. Letitia and I grew up in the same village. I don't mind confessing to you that I once asked her to be my wife. We were so very young, and she was right to refuse me, callow youth that I was with no prospects."

"Really? I don't believe I have ever met anyone who knew Miss Cobb before she came to us," said Sincerity in wonderment. She focused on his hopeful face and smiled again. "And you want me to convince her to grant you a dance, Mr. Boynton?"

"I daresay that would prove impossible, Miss Hartford. But if I might have your permission to call on her? Letitia said she would need your permission in order to receive callers."

Sincerity opened her mouth to tell him that such was not the case, but she hesitated. Perhaps Miss Cobb had a reason for holding Mr. Boynton at arm's length. She looked into his open, honest face and shook her head. More like, it was just Cobbie's shy and retiring nature that was holding her back. Well, she could fix that.

She favored the gentleman with a brilliant smile and said, "Why don't you call on us tomorrow afternoon, Mr. Boynton. Shall we say at three o'clock?"

"Tomorrow? I'm afraid I have business to attend to tomorrow. Would it be too forward of me to suggest Saturday afternoon?"

"Not at all, Mr. Boynton. We will look forward to your call," said Sincerity, feeling very grown-up and in charge of the situation.

"Oh, thank you, Miss Hartford. Thank you ever so much!" he replied, shaking her hand heartily before he hurried away.

Sincerity strolled back to Miss Cobb and sat down beside her, far enough away from Lady Rutherford that she would not be overheard.

"I have met your suitor," she said coyly, keeping her eyes on the couples taking to the floor for the next dance.

"Suitor?" hissed Miss Cobb, glowering at her charge. "I'm sure I don't know what you are talking about."

"No need to play the coquette with me," she teased. "I refer to your Mr. Boynton, of course. Why did you tell him he couldn't call on us and that you couldn't dance with him?"

"I have better things to do with my time than wait on the likes of Giles Boynton," Miss Cobb said haughtily. "I take my duties as your chaperon seriously."

"That's all well and good, Cobbie, but you are certainly allowed to have a life of your own. Besides, I am not a green girl in her first or second Season. I know how to go on."

"Then you must know that it is most improper of us to sit here chatting when you have a young man waiting to lead you into the next set."

Sincerity rose and accepted her next partner's proffered arm. She turned back to Miss Cobb and said sternly, "We will discuss this matter later."

Though the assembly in the Upper Rooms ended at eleven o'clock, Lady Rutherford pressed them to join her for tea, and they accepted, enduring another hour of the old lady's acerbic observations on the people who had attended the assembly and their behavior. Young Lizzie sat in silence, her dark eyes shining with private memories, but Sincerity and Miss Cobb listened politely, nodding at the appropriate moments and giving an occasional, brief response.

By the time Sincerity and Miss Cobb arrived back in Russell Street, they were exhausted and hardly inclined to discuss anything. By unspoken agreement, the ladies sought their beds without broaching the topic of Mr. Boynton or his coming visit.

It occurred to Sincerity that she owed her companion a warning about his call and his interest, but she was unwilling to bring her gentle companion's wrath down upon her head at such a late hour. So she climbed into bed and burrowed into her romantic dreams of Sir Simon. Her fatigue took its toll, however, and she was soon fast asleep.

"Angus, where the devil is my hat? I'm late," shouted Sir Simon, surveying his room suspiciously, as if it had somehow managed to misplace his hat.

"I've got it right here, Major, sir," said the servant, entering the parlor from the bedchamber. "And I sent word t' have yer horse ready and waiting at the front door."

"Thank you, Angus. I may not return until tomorrow. It depends on how long the mill lasts and if there are any beds to be had close to the site of the fight."

"Very good, sir. I'll not be waiting up for you," responded the servant as Simon strode out the door.

Simon was not usually drawn to a fight, but his friends had insisted that he join them, and he didn't want to disappoint them. He would have preferred to spend his day with his pens and sketch pad. He had them with him. He might just pull them out and sketch the fight. On this happy note, Simon hailed the Jackson brothers and Philip Farguson, another former officer who had been with them both on the Peninsula and at Waterloo.

The farther they traveled outside Bath, the more congested were the roads until finally, they took to the fields whenever they could to avoid the carriages and curricles, many of which were driven by young bucks with more hair than wit.

"There's another one," shouted Jackson, pointing back toward the road where another curricle was tilted on its side, one wheel spinning, as the team was led away.

"Fool," said Simon. "Tried to take the corner too fast."

"And probably half bosky to boot," said Farguson, a man who knew and respected horses.

"Surely not. I mean, it's only ten o'clock," commented David Jackson, who tended to think the best of everyone.

"It only takes a sip for some of them," said his brother dispassionately. "Look, there, beyond that next stand of trees. That must be the place."

In the clearing ahead, they could see colorful flags flying from the trees, marking off the area for the mill. It looked as if half the county were already present, and they were glad they were on horseback and would be able to maneuver closer than a curricle could have done. The ring was roped off. Around it there were many good-humored shouts, clapping of backs, and shaking of hands as wagers were placed.

Simon saw an opening and urged Soldier through it, finding himself ringside. He dropped the reins, knowing Soldier was much too well-mannered to move a muscle unless Simon signaled him to do so. Simon reached into the leather pouch attached to the saddle behind him and extracted his pad and pencil. Hastily, he sketched the bustling scene before him.

"Wot's that ye got?" asked a country rustic, staring up at him from his vantage point on the ground.

"Just a sketch of everything," replied Simon.

"Mind if I see?" asked the man.

"Not at all." Simon held the pad down for the man's perusal. "Well?"

Another man, wearing the garb of a country squire, looked over the rustic's shoulder and grinned. Pointing upward, he said, "That's very good, sir, but you forgot the people hanging from that tree up there."

Simon glanced up and laughed. "You're right. I didn't notice them." He hastily added the two young boys who had secured the best vantage point of all, hanging from two stout branches of the huge oak tree that overlooked the makeshift ring. He showed this effort to the squire who grunted his approval.

"Here we go," said Simon as the crowd parted on opposite sides of the ring, and two ham-fisted men, dressed only in breeches, strolled forward.

Simon sketched furiously as they squared off while the crowd cheered, each man having his backers who had placed their wagers accordingly.

"Which one's called the Bruiser?" shouted Simon to his newfound friend.

"The bald one. The other one is called the Hampton Leveler because they say he can level an opponent with one mighty swing."

The crowd's cheers turned surly and insulting as the duo in the ring continued to circle each other, neither one attempting to throw the first punch.

"Come on, ladies," taunted the rustic.

Others picked up the chant, and soon the dissatisfied crowd was as one, taunting and teasing the pugilists.

Simon only laughed, trying to catch the expressions of the two boxers as their concentration shifted from their opponent to the audience.

"There he goes!" shouted the squire, pointing to the Hampton Leveler who wound up for his mighty punch only to connect with air and go spinning out of control.

"Whoa! That'll cost him!" exclaimed the rustic.

The Hampton Leveler regained his balance just in time to turn and meet the Bruiser's fist with his face. He raised his fist to retaliate, and then fell backward, out cold.

"Huzzah!" shouted the Bruiser's supporters.

"Argh!" groaned the Leveler's backers, watching anxiously while the Leveler's men tried to revive him. After a moment, they just shook their heads, and the Bruiser's hand shot up in triumph.

Then the audience fell silent for a moment, the realization hitting each man that the fight was over, the excitement at an end. Some grumbled, while others laughed and clapped everyone on the back as they settled their wagers and left.

Simon found his friends again, and they discussed their options. If they headed back to Bath immediately, they would only get bogged down in the traffic. All of the nearby inns would be crammed with boxing enthusiasts.

"Hallo, sir," called the squire, seeing Simon and his friends.

"Hello, my friend. Are you from these parts?"

"Yes, I live just past this stand of trees."

"Do you know of an inn that might boast a decent enough ale to make a visit worth our trouble?" asked Simon.

"I know of a farm with the best ale in the county, sir. That's mine, and I would be honored if you and your friends would join me."

"That's very kind of you. We don't wish to put you out. Or your good wife," said Simon.

"Well, as to that, there's only me, and I would deem it a privilege, sir, especially if you'd let me have a look at your drawings of the fight."

Simon looked to his friends for confirmation, and they all nodded.

"Then lead on," said Simon, hiding his surprise when the farmer untied a fine-looking bay from the tree and swung into the saddle.

"Quite a nice gelding, Mr. . . . ?"

"Boynton, sir. I'm Giles Boynton. And thank you. I bought him at Tattersall's last year. Couldn't resist."

"Don't blame you. My name is Simon McKendrick." He reached out and shook the farmer's hand. "This is Farguson, and these are the Jackson brothers."

"Nice to make your acquaintance, gentlemen. I think I saw you at the assembly last night."

"Oh, did you go to the assembly?" asked Peter Jackson, his surprise evident.

"Yes, it was the first time I got up the courage to go. I've only lived in this area for a year. I know I may not look it today, but I have a prosperous estate."

"I'm sure young Jackson didn't mean to offer you any insult, Mr. Boynton," said Simon.

"Certainly not. Why, I daresay none of us looks at our best right now. I know I am almost ready to faint with thirst, and I can only applaud our new friend here for taking pity on us," Peter said.

"Here, here!" said his brother David.

"Don't worry. It would take more than that to offend me. And I think I can offer you something more than the finest ale in the county. When I left this morning, my cook was putting a steak pie into the oven that most men would kill for. You'll join me, of course."

"It would be a pleasure."

When they arrived at the spacious manor house, the younger gentlemen could not contain their amazement.

Then Peter said humbly, "We are sorry, Mr. Boynton. We took you for a simple farmer, not a gentleman farmer."

"No need to apologize, my boy. I know it looks quite grand, especially for a bachelor like myself, but it's very comfortable. As I said, I purchased the estate from an old family friend who had no heirs. It was ideal for me since I'm a younger son of a simple country squire. Now all I need is a family to put inside it," he added with a self-deprecating laugh. "Ah, Mrs. Watson, I've brought guests for luncheon. I hope the steak pie is hot."

"Hot and ready, sir. I'll tell th' boy t' add some more settings t' th' table, sir. Won't be above ten minutes."

"Thank you, Mrs. Watson. I've been bragging on your cooking."

"You're too kind," she said, rosy faced with pleasure.

"Why don't we go into the drawing room for something to drink?"

"You're most kind, Mr. Boynton," said Simon, thinking how warm and inviting the house and its master were.

"I don't get many guests. The people hereabouts don't quite know which pigeonhole to put me in, I think." He poured them each a large glass of brandy. "But you promised to allow me to see your drawings, Mr. McKendrick."

"Actually, it's Sir Simon," said Peter.

"Oh, I beg your pardon, Sir Simon. I didn't hear properly."

"That's because I didn't mention it, Mr. Boynton. Actually, it's rather new to me," said Simon, handing his pad to his host.

"He earned it fighting old Boney," supplied David Jackson.

"Then you have my gratitude and respect, Sir Simon. A man who has earned his title will always have my respect," said Boynton, studying Simon's drawings intently. "Oh, I say, this one is really very good. I like the expressions on the contestants."

"Thank you."

"Good, here's lunch. Shall we, gentlemen?"

Their host led the way into the dining room. The sideboard groaned with dishes, the odors wafting toward them, making their stomachs growl in anticipation.

When they had satisfied their appetites, Mr. Boynton took out the drawings again. "You know, the fight was on my land. I've been toying with the idea of making it a regular event, perhaps once each quarter. The innkeepers are keen on it, and I thought it would be a way to bring a bit of prosperity to the village."

"Sounds like a fine idea."

"Capital!" said both the Jackson brothers.

"How are you going to let people know about it?" asked Farguson.

"I hadn't really considered it, but after seeing these . . ." He laid the drawings out on the table and studied them closely again. "Sir Simon, would you sell these to me?"

"Sell them? I'll give them to you, Boynton. You've been an excellent host. We never expected such an excellent repast, or such warm hospitality, when we set out from Bath this morning."

"Thank you. That's very kind of you. But there is one thing. Will you mind if I use these drawings in an advertisement in the paper? I would give you credit for the work, of course."

"That's not necessary."

"Oh, but I want to. They really are quite good. As a matter of fact, I shall probably place an advertisement in the London papers as well as the local one."

"You think they are that good?" asked Simon.

"I believe you could make a living drawing for the newspapers, Sir Simon. I think you could make quite a name for yourself," added Mr. Boynton. "I'm going into Bath tomorrow afternoon on another matter. I shall take these by the newspaper office and see if they would like to use them. A bit of publicity about today's fight wouldn't come amiss."

Simon smiled, inordinately pleased with the praise. He had always enjoyed his pastime, but he had never considered it as anything more than that. Perhaps his doodling was not such a waste of time after all.

\* \* \*

"I do believe June has arrived," said Sincerity, her tone listless.

"It is only May," came the sensible response.

"But it is so warm this afternoon," moaned Sincerity. "I think I will absolutely die if I don't get outside for some fresh air. I think I'll go for a walk."

"You'll do no such thing, miss. Mr. Cooper is supposed to be here within the hour, and I want you here to sign any necessary papers. The sooner we find out where we stand, the better."

As if in answer to her plea, Crispin entered, clearing his throat to gain their attention, and announcing grandly, "Mr. Cooper, ladies."

Miss Cobb rose, but Sincerity remained seated, extending her hand to the elderly gentleman and favoring him with a wan smile.

"You must forgive my charge, Mr. Cooper. It is the heat, I fear. It has brought on a relapse of her lethargy."

"Think nothing of it, Miss Cobb. I am, after all, here to serve Miss Hartford in any way I can."

At his words, Sincerity brightened. Perhaps this wasn't going to be as difficult as she had feared.

"Won't you be seated, Mr. Cooper?" she said sweetly.

"Thank you. Thank you," he replied, taking the large chair on her left. Miss Cobb rejoined Sincerity on the sofa while Mr. Cooper put on his spectacles and opened the case he had brought.

"I know this must seem rather strange, as indeed it is. I am sorry your father is out of the country, Miss Hartford. Indeed, were it for any other client, I would have refused to deal with someone like yourself," he said, still pulling papers from the case.

"A woman, you mean?" asked Miss Cobb.

"No, no, it is not that. But Miss Hartford is in her

minority, you know. One usually deals with her parents or guardians. However, as I said, nothing was as usual where my late client was concerned. According to her will, even though you have not yet reached the age of twenty-five, she provided you access to your own funds. You cannot touch the principal, of course, but the interest in her many investments will be ample for you to live on, Miss Hartford, provided you do not become too extravagant," he added, smiling at her in a fatherly manner. A fully restored Sincerity returned that smile gaily.

"So Miss Hartford may take possession of this house?" asked Cobbie, loudly enough for Crispin, whom she knew was still in the hall listening, to hear.

"Yes, indeed, just as she already has," beamed Mr. Cooper. "Miss Granville was a very astute business-woman. While she allowed me to transact most of her investments for her, she was the one who decided what to buy and sell. I must admit that I have benefited personally from her expertise."

Handing a thick legal document to Sincerity, he pointed out to her the assets—her assets—listed in her great-aunt's will. Her head began to swim with the immense sums of money he claimed each share was worth. Finally, Sincerity pushed the document away, shaking her head.

"Please, Mr. Cooper. I'm afraid I am not the business-woman my late aunt was. While I appreciate your trying to educate me about her invest—"

"Your investments, Miss Hartford. But I understand. As I said before, you may live very comfortably on the interest from your investments. If you wish, I will continue to handle your affairs, just as I did Miss Granville's."

"Yes. Yes. I hope you shall, sir. I, uh, we plan to continue to reside here in Bath, to live quietly," said Sincerity.

Mr. Cooper slapped his knee, giving her an approving grin. "I knew Miss Granville's heir would be every bit as sensible as she was. Your great-aunt assured me that you would want to do just that. She said something about your mother. Well, anyway . . . I won't take up any more of your time," he said, rising. "I'll just leave these papers with you, in case you should want to peruse them later. This very day, I shall set up an account at the bank that you may draw upon for funds."

Sincerity smiled upon him again when he named an exorbitant amount for her pin money. Then she gave her first order, saying firmly, "You will do the same for Miss Cobb."

Miss Cobb protested, but Sincerity would have none of it, insisting that whatever she had was to be shared fully with her friend and companion. Miss Cobb sniffled and blew her nose.

"There's just one more thing, Mr. Cooper. My aunt's house and funds, there's no way they could be taken away from me, is there?" asked Sincerity.

"No, no. Well, that is, I suppose if your father were to want to oversee the estate, he would have that authority. After all, he is still your guardian, until you reach twenty-five. But I'm sure, since he obviously trusts you to be on your own, with your companion, of course, that you needn't suppose he will interfere. Sometimes, when an heir isn't capable of seeing to his own affairs, a guardian will take steps to have him declared incompetent."

The solicitor smiled at his pretty, young client. "But as I said, you have nothing to worry about. Your parents obviously have complete confidence in your ability to manage your own affairs. Let me know if I can be of service to you in any way, ladies."

"One final request, Mr. Cooper. Would you please see to paying our subscriptions to the Master of Ceremonies?"

"I would be happy to do so, Miss Cobb. I'll take care of that this very afternoon. Good day to you."

"Good day," said Miss Cobb. She expelled a long sigh.

"Well, that was most satisfactory, wasn't it, dear? I know you must be relieved. I know I am."

Miss Cobb turned back to Sincerity just in time to catch her as she slumped down on the sofa.

"Crispin!" screamed Miss Cobb.

The butler appeared instantly, moving Sincerity so that her feet were elevated on the arm of the sofa and removing the pillow Miss Cobb had shoved under her head.

"She needs her feet elevated," he explained, kneeling by Sincerity's side and gently tapping her cheeks. "Go and fetch your smelling salts, Miss Cobb. I'll stay with her."

Miss Cobb ran up the stairs, taking them two at a time. She returned a moment later with Trudy and Sam in tow. Sam proceeded to open the windows and both doors to allow a breeze to blow through the room.

"I've brought a cold cloth, Uncle Charles," said Trudy.

"She told me she wasn't feeling well," wailed Miss Cobb, for once allowing someone else to take charge. She bit her lower lip as Crispin waved the smelling salts under Sincerity's nose.

Sincerity blinked, trying to push the vile smell away and sit up.

"Stay still, mistress," said Crispin, gently placing the cool cloth on her smooth forehead.

"What happened?" she whispered pitifully.

"You fainted, my love," supplied Miss Cobb, dabbing at her eyes. "I'm so sorry I didn't believe you when you said you were not well, pet."

"Now, enough of that. Miss Sincerity needs all of us to be quiet and calm, Miss Cobb. You sit down before we have another invalid to tend to," said the butler, his kindly tone robbing his words of insult. Miss Cobb did as he bid, smiling tremulously.

Crispin turned back to his young mistress and asked, "What have you eaten today, Miss Sincerity?"

"I, oh, I don't remember. I don't think I really ate anything. I just didn't feel up to it. My stomach was full of butterflies, waiting for Mr. Cooper to arrive and all."

"Sincerity, it is two o'clock in the afternoon! No wonder you fainted!" exclaimed Miss Cobb.

"Don't be cross with me, Cobbie. I'm sorry."

"Never mind, miss. Sam, go and fetch some of Hervé's cakes and pastries, something with a great deal of sugar in it. And some ale to wash it down," he added.

"Thank you, Crispin. You are most kind," said Sincerity, trying to rise once again. He gently pushed her back, shaking his head.

"I don't know what I would have done without him," said Miss Cobb, smiling down at the butler. His steely eyes met hers, softening just for a second before he turned back to his new mistress.

Sam returned with a pitcher of ale and a glass, followed closely by Hervé who held a plate piled high with pastries for his new mistress.

"I don't think you need have troubled yourself to come, too, Hervé," said Crispin dryly, helping Sincerity sit up, but staying by her side to support her if she needed him.

"Maybe not, but I wanted to make sure these were going to suit mademoiselle," said the Frenchman gruffly.

"They are as wonderful as ever, Hervé. Thank you," said Sincerity, taking another bite.

"Here's a bit of ale, miss," said Sam.

"Thank you, Sam." She swallowed dutifully, smiling at each of them in turn. "I think I am fine now. I'm sorry to have been so much trouble."

"It was no trouble at all," said Crispin, speaking for his staff. "Now, perhaps we can all get back to our duties."

"Yes, Mr. Crispin," they said quickly.

The butler rose, pausing and looking from Miss Cobb to Sincerity and back again. "Please do not hesitate to ring if you need anything, ladies. I shan't be far off."

"Thank you, Crispin," said Sincerity.

"Yes, thank you, Mr. Crispin," said Miss Cobb, lowering her gaze shyly.

"You're most welcome, ladies," he intoned, walking regally out of the room.

Sincerity's eyes flitted from her companion to the butler. Smiling, she watched Miss Cobb fluttering around, dusting the crumbs from the sofa, doing anything to avoid meeting Sincerity's inquiring eyes.

"He is really quite considerate, isn't he?"

"Who? Oh, you mean, Mr. Crispin. Yes, I suppose. What is more to the point, he is very efficient."

"Oh, yes, that must be what you admire about him," teased Sincerity.

"I'm sure I don't know what you mean," said Miss Cobb, her color high.

"Coming it a bit too strong, Cobbie. Methinks the lady doth protest too much," said Sincerity with a giggle.

"That's enough out of you, young lady, causing such a fuss with your silliness. And there you were last night, pretending that my duties to you are all but over!"

"Oh, very well, Cobbie. I was only teasing." She swung her feet to the floor, pausing a moment to be certain the room wasn't going to start spinning.

"Just remember this the next time you are urging me to take up dancing!" said Miss Cobb pertly. "I have no time for such nonsense when I have you to look after, miss."

"Now, Cobbie, I'm sure I . . . Oh no!"

"What is it? Are you feeling faint again?" asked Miss Cobb, rising half out of her seat and calling, "Mr. Crispin!"

"No, no. I'm fine. Really I am," said Sincerity, her face blanching despite her stoic assertions.

"Then what?"

"It's Mr. Boynton!"

"Mr. Boynton? Giles Boynton? What about him?" asked Miss Cobb, suddenly aware that the butler had come running in answer to her summons and was listening.

"I'm afraid I told him he could call on you tomorrow afternoon."

"You did what?" breathed Miss Cobb. "Oh, Sincerity, how could you?"

"Cobbie, I'm sorry. I thought it was for the best. Cobbie! Oh dear, you're not going to faint as well, are you?" she cried when Miss Cobb sank back against the upholstery.

Crispin hurried to Miss Cobb's side, placing his hand on her shoulder for support. Without considering, she put her hand over his, giving his fingers a squeeze.

"I'm fine, I assure you, Crispin. I never faint." She smiled up at him, and he released her shoulder.

"Very good, madam." He turned to Sincerity and asked sharply, "What time may we expect Miss Cobb's gentleman friend?"

"I believe I told him three o'clock," said Sincerity in a small voice, not daring to look Miss Cobb or the censorious butler in the eye.

But Crispin was an expert at hiding his feelings and said appropriately, "Very good, miss. I shall see to it that Hervé has a tea tray ready."

"Thank you, Crispin," said Miss Cobb, the color returning to her face as she gazed up at the butler. "Nothing special, if you please. Mr. Boynton will not be staying long."

From her vantage point, Sincerity could have sworn she saw him smile. Impossible, of course. She had never known him to do so. And why on earth would Crispin care if Miss Cobb had a caller or not? It was not as if he fancied Miss Cobb. What a ridiculous notion that was.

She rose, and Miss Cobb inquired stiffly, "Where do you think you are going, miss?"

"I was going to see if the post had arrived," she fibbed. In reality, she was planning to escape before Miss Cobb could remonstrate her again.

"It has, Miss Hartford," announced Crispin, producing two letters for her before he withdrew.

"Thank you," she said, returning to the sofa and opening the first envelope. After skimming the letter, she handed it to Miss Cobb. "It is from Tranquility in France. She is deliriously happy waiting for the little one to arrive. She wishes we were there, and so on and so forth."

"I wish we could go for a visit, too. Perhaps in the autumn when things are more settled," said Miss Cobb. She smiled at Sincerity, but immediately asked, "What is it? Not more bad news!"

"No, not precisely, Cobbie," replied Sincerity, scanning the second letter again. "My mother wants to know what is going on. She received the one letter from Aunt Prudence. . . ."

"Purportedly from Aunt Prudence," corrected Miss Cobb.

"Yes, but you know what I mean. Now she wants to know how I am faring in my search for a suitable husband. She mentions that she will be paying us a visit if she does not hear from me soon."

"But that would be ruinous," exclaimed Miss Cobb, who could see her career, her livelihood, shattering before her eyes. "You must do something to put her off, Sincerity. Surely you have a contingency plan in the event of such an occurrence!"

"When have you ever known me to plan ahead!" cried Sincerity.

The duo fell silent, one falling into melancholy, the

other busily planning her next outrageous measure. Slowly, a smile formed on Sincerity's rosy lips, traveling upward to wrinkle her pert little nose, before settling in her eyes that began to gleam with amusement.

Watching this transformation, Miss Cobb didn't know whether to clap her hands in relief or turn and run. It didn't matter. Once Sincerity Hartford hatched a scheme, there was no turning back!

# SEVEN

"What the devil is all of this?" demanded Sir Simon, pausing on the threshold of his sitting room at the White Hart Inn, his eyes sweeping the chamber for an intruder. Instead, only his man presented himself, shuffling his feet and looking the very picture of guilt.

"What do you have to say for yourself, Angus?"

"I'm sorry, sir. I had gone out, and Miss Lang must have bribed th' clerk."

"Miss Lang? I might have known. So you didn't have a hand in this?" he asked, looking at the numerous bouquets of flowers.

Angus stifled a sneeze and shook his head vigorously. "Not on your life, Major! I know better than that!"

Simon flicked open the card attached to one bouquet and read the sentimental verse, penned in a delicate script and scented with heavy perfume. On the table was a case of his favorite wine wrapped with a big green bow. The card, again, bore a coy verse.

"I wonder what the deuce possessed her," he muttered.

"As to that, sir, I, uh, did return before Miss Lang left, but I couldn't dissuade her from leaving these, uh, tokens, she called them."

"Tokens of what?" grumbled Simon, entering his bed-chamber and cursing under his breath when he saw yet another vase of brightly colored flowers adorning his nightstand.

"She mentioned something about last night at the assembly, sir. I thought you might understand."

"I understand what a bold little . . . Angus, get me the person who was on duty downstairs when Miss Lang paid her visit. I want a few words with him."

Sir Simon McKendrick considered himself a reasonable man, a civilized man, but having discovered the staff at the White Hart Inn had allowed someone to enter his room in his absence, he found it difficult to curb his temper. His efforts in self-restraint were rewarded when the hapless clerk began to tremble from head to toe.

"What is your name?" Simon demanded, catching his breath.

"Johnson, sir," stammered the young man.

Simon shook his head, looking at the clerk's smooth jaw; it had never seen a razor. The clerk was nothing but a boy. No wonder Miss Lang had been able to have her way. She was perhaps twenty-one herself, but she had learned well her lessons on manipulating the stronger sex. Stronger sex, hah! he thought, taking pity on the trembling clerk.

"Well, Johnson. I shan't report you to the landlord this time if you promise me this will never, ever happen again."

"I promise!" said the youth, his voice breaking into a shrill squeak. "Never again, Sir Simon!"

"Good, then we will say no more about it."

After expending his frustrations on the clerk, Simon turned to his old servant, his temper flaring all over again. But this time, his anger was turned inward. He was the one who had allowed Miss Lang to think he was pursuing her. It had been wrong of him, unworthy of his name.

Oh, she was a beauty, make no mistake. But for him,

dancing with her was no different from dancing with his sister, Jessie. She had told him he could relax with her, could feel free from any of the entanglements one associated with the social intercourse between a man and a woman. But she had deceived him, or perhaps, she had deceived herself. Either way, he would have to let her know she was only a pleasant pastime, like his drawing, but not to be taken seriously. How he hated this awkwardness!

"Angus!" he bellowed. "Clear away these demmed flowers before you start sneezing your head off. And send the wine back to her."

"All of it, sir?" asked the valet forlornly.

"Yes, all of it," he said, stripping off his coat and riding breeches and changing into his kilt. "I'm going for a walk. And if I'm not back before dark, please do not send out a search party. The last time the Jackson brothers came looking for me in the hills, their torches nearly burned down some poor farmer's barn."

"Very good, sir."


"This is the sort of day when I wish I enjoyed riding," said Sincerity, leaning over the half door of the tack room and watching the stableboy polishing the leather harnesses.

"Why don't you, miss?" asked the lad.

"Horses rather frighten me, I suppose," she replied, looking up at the blue sky and sighing.

"I bet old Nate wouldn't frighten you, miss."

"Old Nate?"

"He's sort of out t' pasture. Any road, we don't keep 'im 'ere anymore."

"And he's very gentle?"

"Bout th' best old horse a body could ever want," said the youth. "We keeps 'im at Mr. Goodbody's house on the edge of town 'cause he's got a nice green pasture for old Nate to graze. Sometimes, I go out and ride 'im around a bit. Or I take 'im out to me mum's cottage and give my little sisters a ride. He never takes a fright, never puts a foot wrong."

"Is he very big?" asked Sincerity.

"Oh, no, miss. He's maybe fourteen hands, a nice size for someone small like you er me. Would you like me t' go out and get him? I can bring 'im back in no time."

"Here, now, Tom, what are you doin', talkin' th' mistress's ear clean off?" demanded the heavy-set coachman whose balding head was covered by long strands of thin gray hair.

"No, sir. I'm working," said the boy, making a show of the gleaming brass on the harness.

"I'm afraid I was interrupting him, Mr. Lorrie. He was telling me about old Nate," said Sincerity.

"Ah, that was a good old horse," replied Mr. Lorrie, shaking his head up and down slowly.

"Do you think I might be able to ride Nate? I'm not a very accomplished horsewoman," said Sincerity humbly.

"Anybody can ride Nate, miss. Why, I wouldn't be afraid t' put a newborn babe on top of old Nate. He's that gentle. If you like, I'll send Tom after him. Won't take more than fifteen minutes to fetch him. You can try him out this very afternoon."

"Oh, I . . . Very well. Let's do just that!" said Sincerity, her heart sinking to her stomach at her bold words. But she was not one to back down, so she smiled and went into the house to don her one habit, a simple wool garment in navy.

By the time she had brushed and plaited her hair, put on her half boots, plucked up her courage, and returned to the small stables, Tom and Mr. Lorrie had Nate saddled and waiting.

To the diminutive Sincerity, he looked huge.

"Come right over here, miss. I'll give you a leg up," said the coachman.

"I don't know. Perhaps I should just go for a walk," said Sincerity, looking from the coachman to the horse, and back again.

"Don't be afraid, miss. You'll hurt old Nate's feelings if he thinks yer afraid of 'im," said Tom.

"Very well. I'll try." Closing her eyes, Sincerity let the coachman lift her onto the small horse.

"You need to make sure you're all secure in the saddle, miss. Then take a turn around the yard."

Opening her eyes, Sincerity hooked her knee over the pommel and primly arranged her skirts. She gave a tentative pat to the old horse's neck and smiled at her instructors.

"That's right, miss," said the boy encouragingly.

Nate decided to give his head and neck a vigorous shake, and Sincerity dropped the reins, her eyes wide with terror.

"Now, now, it's nothing to be afraid of, miss. He's just letting you know he's ready to go wherever you want to send him."

"I don't think . . . That is . . ."

"Tom, why don't you go and saddle your pony and accompany Miss Hartford for a little ride." He gave her foot a little pat, adding, "It will do you good, and this is nothing like London, miss. You can go straight out into the country for a quiet ride with nobody to bother you or old Nate. You'll like that, won't you, old boy?"

Nate snorted his response, and Sincerity gave a nervous giggle.

"You really think he is safe?" she asked doubtfully.

"As safe as a comfortable chair by th' fire, miss. You'll find old Nate is a real gentleman."

"Are you ready, miss?" asked the eager boy.

"As ready as I shall ever be."

Sincerity and Nate followed, ambling along after Tom and his younger pony who led the way out of Bath and along winding roads to the cliffs overlooking the city.

"How are you doing, miss?" called the boy.

"We're fine," she replied, smiling when she realized that she was indeed feeling comfortable while on horseback. It was a novel sensation. She patted Nate's neck, and he gave a pleased snort.

"I thought you might like t' see th' view from up here," said Tom, pulling back on the reins and allowing Sincerity and Nate to come abreast of him.

The vista before her took Sincerity's breath away. The late-afternoon sun shining through a few low-lying clouds bathed the city below them with golden streaks of light. A haziness added to its fairy-tale quality, and Sincerity could only stare raptly at the scene.

"Would you mind moving a bit to the right, lass?" said a deep, lilting voice.

Sincerity's dreamworld shattered as she recognized the voice, and she twisted in the saddle, but her sudden movement was too much, even for Nate's affable disposition. He stepped daintily to the side. Sincerity dropped the reins and grabbed for the pommel, shutting her eyes tightly.

"It's all right, miss. He's not going anywhere," said Sir Simon, shading his eyes against the sun as he patted Nate's glossy neck. He retrieved the reins and handed them back to Sincerity's trembling hands. She shook her head, closing her eyes again.

"She's not much of a rider," supplied the groom.

"So I see," said Simon, grinning at the boy. "Would you like to get down for a while, miss? Just to give you a chance to get your poise back. I don't think this old fellow is going anywhere in a hurry, but you never can tell."

"Yes, I think I would like that. Thank you, Sir Simon."

"Ach, so you know my name?" he said, keeping his voice smooth and calm, as if speaking to a frightened child. It was odd that he couldn't place her. He was usually quite good with faces. She was very young, of course. Perhaps sixteen or seventeen, he judged. Her dark wool habit, buttoned tightly to the throat, was that of a schoolgirl, loose-fitting with very straight lines. And like a girl, she wore only a small cap on top of her head with long braids trailing down her back.

"Yes, I happened to overhear it . . . in the Pump Room, I believe," said Sincerity, relieved that he didn't recognize her as the vain young lady at the assembly or the clumsy goose from the booksellers.

"Then you have the better of me, Miss . . . ?"

"Hartford, sir. And I am sorry to be such a goose," she said, her smile putting the sun to shame—or so Simon thought.

"Not at all. It was getting a bit late to be drawing anyway," he replied with a smile.

He reached up to pluck her off her horse. Perhaps she was not so very young after all, he decided, looking up at her engaging face as his hands encircled her tiny waist. It was the childish habit and the braids that had fooled him. But with those curves, she was certainly not a child.

Suddenly Simon recalled what engaging in civil conversation with a young lady had provoked with a certain Miss Lang. Alarms sounded in his head, and he would have released Miss Hartford if it wouldn't have caused her to fall on her face.

What if she had not just happened along? What if this young woman knew about his forays to the cliffs and was trying to entrap him? Frowning mightily, he quickly completed his task, dropping his hands immediately.

Sincerity, being lifted gently to the ground, didn't notice his change of mood, and when she had her feet firmly planted on the ground, she smiled at him again, her blue eyes wide and innocent. His nostrils breathed in the hint of lavender from her hair.

"Thank you," she said, her voice a mere whisper, wishing he had not been so quick to release her. Her skin still quivered where his hands had been.

"Oh, think nothing of it," he replied blithely, tossing the reins of the horse to Tom who led him away, and promising himself he would not encourage her. But this resolution exploded like a flash of lightning when he looked into those eyes.

"Do you come up here often?" asked Simon, stepping away from her and strolling toward the edge of the cliff. Of course she did not, he told himself crossly. If she did, he would certainly have noticed her. It was not as if there were a constant parade of beautiful young ladies in this out-of-the-way spot.

Sincerity hung back, eyeing the edge cautiously. "No. This is my first time to venture into the countryside. It is quite beautiful," she added, wondering where her feminine skills had flown to just because she was in the presence of this handsome man.

The fact that she had been filling every spare moment weaving fanciful tales about him was neither here nor there. Those were daydreams, and she never confused them with real life. So what on earth was the matter with her? She could almost believe that he had some magical power over her. But that was absurd, and she had too much social expertise to be speaking like a veritable schoolgirl!

"I think it is the best part of visiting Bath. Come closer. You can see the spire of the abbey over there," he said, turning and holding out a hand to her. Resolution be damned!

Sincerity craned her neck, but she didn't move any closer. She glanced at his long, strong fingers and willed herself to take his hand, but she couldn't move. Frowning fiercely, she cursed her old weakness.

"Is something the matter? I don't bite, you know," he said crossly. *What is the matter with the chit? Surely she is not afraid of me!*

She grimaced and confessed, "I am not casting aspersions on your manners, Sir Simon, but there is something that terrifies me even more than horses, and that is high cliffs. Where I grew up, there are tall white cliffs overlooking the English Channel. As a child, I developed a terror of falling into the sea. As a matter of fact, just seeing you so close to the edge makes me nervous."

"I wouldn't let you slip," he said, cocking his head to one side. It was unusual to find such candor in a young lady of fashion. He rather liked it and the fact that she was worried for his safety.

"I'm afraid your reassurance is not enough. I simply cannot persuade my feet to take me a step closer. I am sorry. I don't mean to be rude," said Sincerity, praying for a sudden cloudburst, anything to end this awkwardness.

She looked into his eyes, willing him to understand. The warmth of his gaze should have made her blush, but instead, she was overcome with a calm serenity, as if he were lending her courage. She took a step closer, then closed her eyes. With a small chuckle, he joined her, safely away from the edge.

"There, is that better?" he asked. Sincerity smiled up at him gratefully, and he added, "I don't think you're rude, Miss Hartford. I applaud such forthrightness."

"You are very kind to say so," she replied, expelling her pent-up breath. Trying for a topic of normalcy, she asked, "What brings you up here, Sir Simon?"

"I like to come up to the cliffs to escape all the hustle and bustle. I find people rarely notice the beauty of

places where they live. It's good to be alone from time
to time, to be able to take it all in."

"And here I am disturbing you. I'm so sorry. I'll go
away immediately," she said, gazing up at his handsome
face for one last look before turning away.

"No, no, I didn't mean you, Miss Hartford. You are
not disturbing me in the least," he said, surprised to realize that while her presence on the cliffs was not a dis-
turbance, she was disturbing to him.

Sincerity looked down, confused by the warmth and
admiration in his gray eyes. While he had been walking
through her dreams every night since the first time she'd
seen him, she wasn't certain that she wanted a real flirta-
tion with him. It would only complicate matters.

She glanced up again and thought how wonderfully
handsome he was. He raised his brows quizzically, and
she looked away.

Noticing his drawing pad on the green grass, Sincerity
nodded toward it and asked, "Are you an artist?" Anything to return to less intimate topics.

"I would never make such a claim," he said with a
self-deprecating chuckle, "but I do enjoy it."

"May I see your sketches?"

Simon didn't know what possessed him, but he acqui-
esced immediately and began flipping through the pages.
Normally, these drawings were private. They were
sketches of his home in Scotland, of his family. But he
found himself explaining every detail, every stroke of
the pen, wanting to make her see the beauty of his home
through his eyes.

"They are wonderful," said Sincerity when she had
seen all of them, and he was putting them away. "I was
always such a disappointment to Mr. Ross, the drawing
master my mother hired. I know a young lady is supposed to have some sort of talent—watercolors, sketches,
needlework—but I never quite got the knack of any of

it. You would have pleased Mr. Ross to no end," she finished, her blue eyes twinkling.

"I'm sure you exaggerate, but thank you for the compliment." He looked up at the sky and added, "It is getting late. I don't wish to detain you."

"No, of course not," she said glumly. She was enjoying their conversation too much to want it to end, but she signaled to Tom, grimacing as he led the old horse forward. If there were some other way to get home, she would have jumped at it.

"Allow me to help you," said Sir Simon, placing his hands on her waist and lifting her effortlessly into the saddle. He couldn't help but notice her trembling, and he said, "My sister always hums when she rides. She finds it calms both her and her mount. You might give it a try, Miss Hartford."

"Thank you, Sir Simon. I shall," said Sincerity, pulling on one rein and turning Nate toward home. She couldn't tell him, of course, that it was as much his touch that had set her to trembling as it was her fear of riding.

As for Sir Simon, he told himself to just let her go, but he couldn't refrain from calling after her, "Perhaps we will meet again, Miss Hartford."

"Perhaps," called Sincerity without looking back, unwilling to risk a fall by letting go of the pommel.

Besides, she would be seeing him that night in her dreams.


"Have you decided what to do about your mother's letter?" asked Miss Cobb when she and her charge were alone in the cozy sitting room that separated their bedchambers. "I know we cannot possibly keep your aunt's demise a secret until you reach your majority, but I had hoped we might survive the summer without a visit."

"Perhaps we shall. I have written her another letter, this time, of course, as myself."

"And how is that going to keep her at bay?" asked Miss Cobb.

"You know all my mother wants is for me to find a suitable suitor. So I have!" said Sincerity with a grin.

"Have what?"

"Have found a suitable suitor."

"Who? I don't recall anyone paying you particular attention last night at the assembly. And I am certain no gentlemen have called on us here. Do not tell me you have been having clandestine assignations with someone?" complained Miss Cobb.

"How you do go on, Cobbie. Do you want to hear the letter or not?" demanded Sincerity, producing the letter and unfolding it carefully.

"Oh, very well, but I hate to be a party to such deceit."

"Nevertheless?"

"Yes, yes, go on and read it to me," said Miss Cobb, nervously tying and untying knots in her lace handkerchief.

"You will be happy to know that all is well here in Bath. I have made the acquaintance of several unexceptional ladies who have introduced me to the most proper gentlemen."

"Don't you think that's doing it up a bit too brown, Sincerity?" said Miss Cobb.

"No, I don't. I am speaking of Lady Rutherford, you know."

"Well, won't your mother wonder why your great-aunt hasn't been introducing you to people?"

"Ah, I mentioned in the first paragraph that she is not feeling very strong, and so has not taken me about as she had planned. I sort of hinted that she had given me over to the care of some other older sponsor."

"Very well. Continue."

"I have made the acquaintance of one gentleman in particular. I hesitate to mention his name this early, but suffice it to say that he is Sir S_. I know you will approve. He has a large estate up north and is somewhat older than I am. Miss Cobb thinks he has had a steadying influence on me. He is tall, like Papa. He is also a talented artist, though it is merely an amusement.

I remain your dutiful daughter. . . ."

"There! What do you think?"

"Is that all?" asked Miss Cobb.

"I should think there is enough information there to keep Mother interested and curious, but there is nothing in the letter to cause her alarm. She won't want to leave London at this time, so she will use this as an excuse not to visit. I haven't made his identity too transparent, have I?"

"I have no idea who this person is. I thought it was just someone you made up," said Miss Cobb.

"So much the better. I know Mother will eventually show up on our doorstep, but the longer I can postpone the inevitable, the better."

"I can't quibble over that!" exclaimed Miss Cobb, stifling a yawn. "Now, I really am tired, my dear. It has been quite an eventful day what with Mr. Cooper's visit and all. I think I'll go to bed early."

"Yes, you must get your beauty sleep for tomorrow," teased Sincerity, forgetting for a moment that Miss Cobb was still a little miffed with her over inviting Mr. Boynton to tea.

"What I must do, is get enough sleep to keep up with you, young lady. I suggest you go to sleep, too. We have Lady Rutherford's card party tomorrow night, remember?"

"Yes, I remember. Good night, Cobbie."

"Good night, my dear."

Sincerity blew out the candles and trudged into her

own room, removing her wrapper and crawling into bed. There was a full moon, and it cast long shadows on the walls, but Sincerity was not one to create fanciful fears. She was very sensible about such things. Flights of the imagination were for more pleasant fancies.

She pulled up the covers, turning on her side and closing her eyes. Yes, there he was on the cliffs, wearing his dark green kilt, his tawny hair unrestrained by that black ribbon. He was calling her name as she rode *ventre à terre* to his side. And this time, when he took her in his arms, she knew how it felt, that tingling and aching the mere touch of his hands could produce.

Smiling, Sincerity fell asleep.

Across town, Sir Simon sat hunched over his cards, studying his friends' faces for telltale clues before placing his next wager. He took another long pull on his brandy. He had been losing badly all night, something he rarely did when he played against this crew; they were all so predictable.

But tonight he was distracted by the face of an angel with golden curls and an impish smile. He shook his head at such nonsense. Perhaps this city had bewitched him.

"Devil take you, Farguson!" he muttered, throwing in his cards while his friend raked in the pot.

"Not up to your usual game, Simon," commented Farguson.

"I think his mind's on a tall, red-haired beauty," quipped Jackson, shuffling the deck.

"Devil take you, too," said Simon, grinning. He knew if he protested, the others would never believe him. And he wasn't about to reveal to them that his thoughts were being stolen by a mere slip of a girl whose hair was the color of sunshine.

He hoped she would return the next afternoon. If she did, she would find him waiting.

"Well, that was certainly uncomfortable," said Miss Cobb when Mr. Boynton finally took his leave of them.

"I know, Cobbie. I'm sorry I invited him. He made it sound like you two were old friends."

"In a way, I suppose we are. And it was nice to talk about old times. We did grow up in the same village, and Giles was always kind to me, even though my family was quite poor."

"He seems to have done rather well for himself," said Sincerity.

"Indeed he has, if he is to be believed," said Miss Cobb.

"Is there any reason to doubt him?" asked Sincerity.

"No, not really. I know his family estate went to his older brother, but there was also a great deal of money. There is no reason to suppose he didn't inherit some of that and buy his estate."

"But?" prodded Sincerity.

"But I prefer to make my own choices, Miss Impudent," said Miss Cobb, wagging a finger at her former pupil. "From now on, if I choose to invite someone to call, I will. Until then, please refrain from acting on my behalf."

"I will, Cobbie. And again, I am sorry. I thought it was for the best. I certainly didn't mean to upset you."

"No harm done. It was pleasant to talk about old times, but I don't want to encourage him."

"That will make tonight difficult, since he was also invited to Lady Rutherford's."

"We'll speak no more about that. By the way, did you post that letter?"

"Yes, I did, first thing this morning."

"I was wondering . . . Do you think I should write to your mother? After all, I am your chaperon. I could put in a good word for your Sir S."

"No, no. I don't want her to think a betrothal is imminent. That really would bring her to Bath posthaste. No, I think it best if I do all the writing, both from me and from Aunt Prudence."

Miss Cobb groaned.

"Never mind, Cobbie. Let's go upstairs and decide what we are going to wear to Lady Rutherford's card party tonight."

"I am going to wear that pale gold gown I purchased in London last year."

"Oh, that's lovely with your coloring. What shall I wear? I love that cherry-striped gown, but do you think it is a little too bold?" asked Sincerity when they had entered her room. The gown in question was lying across her bed, the matching silk slippers beside it.

"Not at all. It is charming, with the ivory bodice and sleeves. You should wear that ruby stickpin your father had made into a pendant on an ivory ribbon."

"What a good idea. I haven't had a chance to wear that before. I believe I'll . . ." There was a knock on the door. "Come in. Trudy, I need an ivory ribbon. See if you . . . Oh, Crispin. I didn't realize it was you."

"I am sorry to disturb you, miss, but this has just arrived from Mr. Cooper." He entered the room and placed a black leather case on the dressing table.

"Whatever could it be?" asked Sincerity, crossing the room and trying to open the case.

"Here is the key, miss. Shall I?" asked the butler.

"Yes, thank you, Crispin. Oh, my! Cobbie, come and see. Where did these come from?"

"These were Miss Granville's. She loved to collect jewelry. There are some very elegant and expensive pieces, I believe. Others were more of a sentimental value," said the butler, moving toward the door. "Will there be anything else?"

"That's all, Crispin. Thank you."

"Only look at this necklace with the heart-shaped locket, Cobbie. Isn't it pretty? I wonder if there is a lock of hair inside it," said Sincerity with a giggle. She opened the locket, but nothing fell out. Instead, painted in vivid colors, was a tiny miniature of a young man with thick black hair.

"Now, who do you suppose this is?" she asked, showing the picture to Miss Cobb.

"No one I've ever seen," said Miss Cobb.

"Nor I. I think there was more to my great-aunt than any of us ever knew." Sincerity slipped the locket into its velvet pouch and returned it to the case. Picking up another necklace, she asked, "What is that stone called?"

"Topaz, I think. Isn't that pretty?" said Miss Cobb.

"Oh, Cobbie, this would be perfect with your gold gown, the one you are wearing tonight."

"Yes, but I couldn't wear your jewelry, Sincerity. That's part of your inheritance."

"I'm not asking you to keep it, just to borrow it. It will be the perfect accessory," said Sincerity, moving behind Miss Cobb and putting the necklace around her neck. "Well?"

"Oh, very well. Thank you, Sincerity. You are always so generous."

"Me? It is very kind of you to say so, but . . ."

"But it is true," said Miss Cobb, turning and giving her former pupil a quick hug. "You don't have a selfish bone in your body."

"I daresay Mother would not agree with that assessment," Sincerity said dryly. "Nevertheless, thank you. Now, I'll ring for Trudy so we can get ready for Lady Rutherford's. I do hope they know I never lose at cards . . . not to anyone."

# EIGHT

"May I present Sir Simon McKendrick, Lady Rutherford?" asked Mr. Jackson.

"What? Oh, yes, this is the one you told me about. Can you play cards, young man?" she asked with one of her wheezing cackles.

"With the best of them," replied Jackson.

"Let him speak for himself," she said, giving the young man's arm a sharp rap with her lorgnette.

Simon laughed and replied, "Yes, my lady, though I don't particularly like to win money from ladies."

"Are you any good at cards?" she demanded, raising her lorgnette to her eyes and raking him from head to toe with a contemplative stare.

Simon laughed out loud and nodded. "One doesn't like to boast, my lady, but I am considered a worthy opponent."

"Hmph, then you can be my partner, Sir Simon. At least that way you won't be winning any money from your hostess. We'll take that table over there. Lizzie," she called, forcing her granddaughter to look up in alarm. "Quit making sheep's eyes at Mr. Jackson and see to the rest of our guests. I'm going to play cards."

"Yes, Grandmother," said the girl, turning scarlet. Then Jackson whispered something in her ear, and she giggled.

Ignoring the young people, Lady Rutherford dragged her prey forward, taking her seat at the table, saying, "This is Miss Cobb. And I've forgotten your name," she added, staring at the gentleman seated opposite Miss Cobb.

"Giles Boynton, my lady," said the squire, shaking hands with Sir Simon. This evening, Mr. Boynton was resplendent in a high collar that restricted the movement of his head, and his cravat was tied to perfection. His coat was dark purple, a color that only served to accent his sallow complexion.

"I'm already acquainted with Mr. Boynton," said Sir Simon before turning his attention to Miss Cobb. "But I have not had the pleasure before, ma'am."

"How do you do, Sir Simon? I take it from your accent that you are not a native of Bath, either," said Miss Cobb.

"No, only visiting."

"Then you have friends here. How nice."

"I'm afraid my friends merely met me here. No, to be quite truthful, my physician advised I come to Bath for a change of scenery."

"You don't look sick," observed Lady Rutherford, once again raising her lorgnette.

"No, I'm not ill. I just needed a change. What about you, Miss Cobb? Are you a resident?"

"Only just recently, Sir Simon."

"Wasn't that lucky for me!" said Mr. Boynton, jumping back into the conversation. "Miss Cobb and I are childhood friends. I was delighted to discover her here in Bath. Yes, sir, I'm a really lucky fellow."

"Yes, wasn't that lucky?" said Miss Cobb, not quite managing to hide her dismay.

Sir Simon shot her a quizzical look and changed the conversation, receiving a grateful smile from Miss Cobb. "Did you take those sketches of mine to the newspaper?"

"Yes, indeed, I did. He was very pleased with them.

He sent two of them on to a friend at the *Morning Post* in London. You should see the drawing Sir Simon did of . . . My dear Letitia, is anything the matter? You've turned white as a sheet!" Mr. Boynton exclaimed, reaching across the table and touching Miss Cobb's cheek.

She drew back automatically, but her eyes never left Sir Simon's face. Sir S! It had to be! And he was an artist! An older man—Well, as to that, she judged him to be in his early thirties, but Sincerity would, of course, consider that old.

"Miss Cobb, are you all right?" asked Sir Simon.

"Take some wine," snapped Lady Rutherford, who had grown tired of the conversation in the first place and certainly didn't want this companion to become the focus of attention at her card party.

"I beg your pardon," said Miss Cobb, dropping her gaze to regain her composure. Taking a deep breath, she looked up, smiling politely at the trio surrounding her. "A momentary lapse. Now, shall we play whist?"

"If you wish," said Sir Simon, handing the deck of cards to Boynton to prevent him from continuing a conversation the lady obviously wanted to forget.

Her attention on the square of people at the table across the room, Sincerity played one wrong card after another. She knew without being told that her companion had guessed at the identity of Sir Simon. She also knew that she could not face Miss Cobb's questions about how they had met, how she knew about Sir Simon's artistic pastime.

"My goodness, Sincerity, I thought you said you were a skilled player," teased Lizzie, feeling very grown-up with the handsome Mr. Jackson and the sophisticated Mr. Farguson on either side of her.

"I'm afraid my mind has been wandering this evening. I apologize, Mr. Farguson," Sincerity said to her partner.

"No matter. It is just as much my fault," he replied.

"It is very gallant of you to say so, but I know you must be wishing you had chosen someone else for a partner."

"Not at all, Miss Hartford."

"Philip isn't a very good player, either," said Mr. Jackson. "Of course, he's better when he isn't distracted by two such beautiful young ladies."

Lizzie giggled and tapped his arm with her cards, her flirtatious gesture losing its effect as the cards flipped out of her grasp and scattered across the polished floor.

"Oh, no!" she wailed, ready tears springing to her eyes.

"There, there, Miss Montfort. Please do not distress yourself. No harm done," said Mr. Jackson, patting at Lizzie's arm while Mr. Farguson retrieved the cards.

Sincerity noticed that crying did not improve Lizzie's looks. Her skin instantly turned splotchy, and her eyes were red and swelling rapidly. Mr. Jackson, however, didn't seem to mind. He looked ready to take the girl into his arms.

"Don't cry, Miss Lizzie," said Mr. Jackson.

Mr. Farguson, who had better sense than his friends, gave a hearty laugh and said bracingly, "Of course she will not cry. Miss Montfort has more sense than that! Now, let's resume our game. No more of your tactics to make me and Miss Hartford lose our concentration, Jackson."

"Yes, Mr. Farguson and I are wise to your tricks," said Sincerity, taking her cue.

Lizzie smiled, dabbing her eyes with the handkerchief Mr. Jackson had given her. "I suppose I was just being silly."

"Of course you were, my, uh, Miss Montfort. After all, you're among friends here," said Mr. Jackson.

"You're right," she replied, her smile for him alone.

She handed him the handkerchief, but he pushed it

away, saying cleverly, "You had better keep it handy for our opponents. After this hand, the game will be ours."

"We shall see about that," replied Sincerity with a laugh.

But as the play continued, she had to admit to herself that it was impossible for her to concentrate on the cards with Sir Simon in the same room. It was also impossible for Sincerity to admit that she was of two minds about what had her so agitated: the possibility that Sir Simon might speak to her, or the possibility that he might not. If he happened to glance her way while she was seated with Lizzie, she was sure he would remember their exchange at the assembly, that he would recognize her for that vain young lady. But if he did not notice her, would she not feel more stricken?

That was the problem with real life, she thought dismally. One could never be certain how other people were going to act. It wasn't like that in her daydreams where she had control over the people! That was why she preferred them to these real situations. That was why she had sworn not to wed. Then she would never have to worry about pleasing a husband. She'd had a lifetime of trying to please others. Now it was her turn!

So really, she told herself firmly, it didn't matter what Sir Simon did or didn't do this evening!

"This trick takes the hand, and that's the rubber!" announced Mr. Jackson.

Sincerity sent her partner a remorseful little smile, but conversation was suspended as Lady Rutherford's butler announced that the buffet supper was waiting in the dining room.

Lizzie gave a happy little trill and rose. Sincerity and the two gentlemen pushed back from the table as well.

"Let's go in while everyone else is finishing their games," said Lizzie eagerly. "I want you to sample the trifle, Mr. Jackson. I helped prepare it," she added proudly.

Sincerity and Mr. Farguson exchanged amused glances, detecting Mr. Jackson's alarm at Lizzie's domestic revelation.

Her partner offered her his arm, leaning down and whispering, "He looks rather like an animal being backed into a corner."

"Yes, or a mouse who see traps everywhere he steps," replied Sincerity with a quiet laugh.

"Parson's mousetraps, you mean."

"Precisely," she responded, feeling very much in harmony with Mr. Farguson, who was a pleasant man of perhaps twenty-seven years. He had light brown hair, dark eyes, and a ready smile, but he was not the gadabout that his friend Peter Jackson was.

Their path took them past Lady Rutherford's table, where play was serious and the four occupants of the table were too absorbed to notice anyone else. Sincerity breathed a sigh of relief that she would not have to confront Sir Simon yet. Perhaps, she thought, they will not even break for supper!

Had Sincerity seen Sir Simon raise his eyes when she passed, his nostrils flaring as he caught a familiar scent, she would not have felt so sanguine. He turned, watching her disappear through the drawing-room doors, one brow cocked skyward. The hair was piled on top of her head in an elegant style, but the figure was the same. His hands remembered that shapely waist, and his nose had not forgotten the sweet hint of lavender that clung to her.

But surely this was not the sweet, shy girl he had met on the cliffs. This girl was a young lady of fashion. He frowned suddenly as he recalled where they had met before—at the bookseller's and the assembly! She was the one telling her friend—Lady Rutherford's granddaughter, now that he thought about it—how to forestall dancing with some poor chap she happened to find boring. He couldn't recall her precise words, but he remembered being chilled by the way she had coldly consigned the hapless man to the devil rather than spend another moment in his tiresome company.

It was impossible to reconcile the two personalities—the sweet innocent of the cliffs and the calculating social butterfly of the assembly. Unless, he thought, his eyes narrowing as she smiled up at something his friend Farguson had said, the meeting at the bookseller's and on the cliffs had been staged. Perhaps Miss Hartford was the worst kind of female, one who would do all she could to ensnare a husband. Since he hadn't fallen for the staged meeting at the bookseller's, she might have arranged to meet him on the cliffs. Perhaps like Miss Lang, Miss Hartford had bribed the clerk at the White Hart to discover his direction.

He had to admit he had been intrigued by the sweet innocence of the girl on the cliffs. She had seemed so sincere in her fears of horses and heights. It had probably all been an act, he scoffed, all for his benefit.

Not that it mattered, of course. It would take more than a brief touch, the lifting of a girl from the saddle, to burn her into his memory.

"It is your play, Sir Simon," snapped the cantankerous Lady Rutherford.

"Of course," he replied smoothly, laying down his card.

Lady Rutherford chortled happily. "We've got you now, Boynton!"

The remainder of the cards were played quickly, and Sir Simon rose, offering his arm to Miss Cobb, leaving Boynton for Lady Rutherford. It wasn't the proper thing to do, of course, but then, he didn't care much about the proprieties after spending two hours with his hostess.

"She will be very cross with you," whispered Miss Cobb.

"Lady Rutherford? I really don't care, unless you would have preferred Mr. Boynton's escort," he added devilishly.

"You know I would not, Sir Simon. I'm afraid I am not a very good actress. I think you saw right through me."

"You were good enough to fool Boynton, and that's all that polite manners require, isn't it?" They paused on the threshold of the dining room, and Simon asked, "Would you care to be seated and allow me to fetch you a plate?"

"You're most considerate, Sir Simon," said Miss Cobb, dropping his arm when he would have led her toward the tables scattered against the far window that overlooked the gardens. "If you will take care of the food, I will endeavor to find an inconspicuous place for us to sit."

She walked toward the window, smiling at the beautiful backdrop Lady Rutherford had provided for her guests. Beyond the tables inside, others were set up on the limestone terrace to allow guests to enjoy the mild evening. The gardens were lighted with miniature Chinese lanterns that swayed in the soft breeze. She saw Sincerity sitting at one of the tables outside and prepared to join her.

"Where shall we sit, Miss Cobb?" asked Lady Rutherford, appearing suddenly with Mr. Boynton in tow.

Letitia Cobb didn't often think about the life she led, always putting other people's considerations before her own. But with the bitter old woman staring at her through that gold lorgnette, she wanted to tell her she didn't care where either of them sat, as long as it was nowhere near her!

Instead, turning away from the young people, she forced a smile and said, "Why don't we join those people at the far table?"

"The duchess?" Lady Rutherford grimaced and shook her head.

"Is she really a duchess?" asked the awestricken Mr. Boynton.

"No, you daft man! I just call her that because she acts like she is one half the time."

"Then why did you invite her to your card party?" he asked.

"You don't really know too much about society, do you?" she snapped. "You have to invite everybody of importance, even if you can't stand the sight of them."

Mr. Boynton looked to Miss Cobb for confirmation of this, but she was not paying attention to the exchange.

"Where is Sir Simon? I thought he was with you," said Lady Rutherford.

"He went to fetch our plates."

"Should have told a footman to do that, just like I did," complained the old lady, frowning as she stared at her crowded dining room. "There are too many people in here. Come with me. We'll take our plates back to the drawing room and use our card table for a dining table."

"If you wish," said Miss Cobb, not caring any longer where they sat. She envisioned a very long evening.

"Miss Cobb, could you please come and settle an argument," said Sincerity, appearing at her friend's elbow.

"Very well, if you need me," she replied.

"Oh, we do, we do. You're the only one who can help," Sincerity replied, loudly enough for Mr. Boynton and Lady Rutherford to hear as she turned Miss Cobb toward her new acquaintances.

"Won't you excuse me for a few minutes, my lady, Mr. Boynton? I must tend to my charge," she explained, hoping she had managed to keep the relief out of her voice.

As Sincerity propelled Miss Cobb toward the terrace, she whispered, "I could not stand by and watch you dragged back into her clutches. She is entirely too possessive of you. I do believe I am beginning to dislike our hostess."

"Sincerity!" said Miss Cobb, but she could not truthfully protest Sincerity's unkind remark. She was much too pleased with her unexpected respite from Lady Rutherford—and Mr. Boynton.

Before they joined the others, Miss Cobb said quietly, "Sir Simon will be joining us, too, Sincerity. Will that make you too uncomfortable?"

"Why should that make me uncomfortable?" she asked airily.

Miss Cobb leaned close to her ear and whispered, "I know he is the suitor you wrote your mother about."

"And what has that to say to the matter? I had to choose someone real to add the ring of truth to my description. It just happened to be Sir Simon. I don't even know the man."

"Oh, that's a relief, then. I was worried. . . . But I can see I need not have done so. Oh, here he comes now."

Simon nodded to his friends and placed two plates on the table before holding out a chair for Miss Cobb, ignoring Sincerity completely. Mr. Farguson performed the same service for Sincerity, and she pasted a brittle smile on her face.

He had remembered her.

"Ladies, this is Sir Simon McKendrick. Sir Simon, my friend, Miss Sincerity Hartford, and our hostess's granddaughter, Miss Lizzie Montfort."

"How do you do?" asked Sir Simon, nodding congenially to Lizzie Montfort and avoiding looking at Sincerity. Turning his attention back to Miss Cobb, he added, "And do you know my friends, Mr. Jackson and Mr. Farguson?"

"Yes, I met them at the assembly," replied Miss Cobb. "Good evening, gentlemen."

"Good evening, Miss Cobb. How are you two faring with Lady Rutherford?" asked Mr. Jackson. He quickly added for Lizzie's sake, "She must be a formidable opponent."

"You needn't quibble about plain speaking where my grandmother is concerned, Mr. Jackson," said Lizzie. "I know she is very outspoken."

"I only meant to say that since she absolutely terrifies me, Miss Lizzie, I wouldn't want to play against her," he responded smoothly. "I much prefer her granddaughter."

Miss Cobb decided the conversation was bordering on the improper and said, "Her ladyship is Sir Simon's partner, so he is faring very well, indeed. I am a very mediocre card player myself, unlike Sincerity here. I felt sorry for you and Miss Montfort, Mr. Jackson. I hope Sincerity and Mr. Farguson did not take all your money."

"Quite the contrary. Miss Hartford and Mr. Farguson gave up almost every hand."

"You surprise me," said Miss Cobb, staring at her former pupil as if she could see right through her. Sincerity pretended a great interest in her food. "Sincerity is usually quite a dab hand at cards. Something must be distracting her this evening."

"Perhaps it is the company. Perhaps they are not stimulating enough," said Sir Simon.

His lips were smiling, but there was no amusement in his eyes, and Sincerity's heart plunged to new depths. He had remembered her from the assembly, the way she had coldly described to Lizzie how to avoid meeting up with that boring man with the pigs.

"Now you are being too naughty," giggled Lizzie, unfurling a fan and fluttering it in front of her face.

Sincerity flashed her new friend a warning glance before smiling sweetly at Sir Simon and saying pointedly,

"I daresay my luck is out this evening all the way around."

"I understand," he responded. "It must be quite difficult for someone as, uh, world-weary as you are, Miss Hartford, to find amusement in a quiet watering spot like Bath. The company must seem a trifle dull."

"Dull? Certainly not, Sir Simon. Some of it is decidedly unsettling. People behave the same everywhere, I think. They are sometimes kind, sometimes heartless. The problem is you can never know which face they will be wearing," she replied sweetly while the others around the table gasped.

"Now, if you will excuse me, I have the headache. I hate to cut short this delightful tête-à-tête, but do you think we might go home, Miss Cobb?" She pushed away from the table with its heaping plates of delicacies, and rose, causing all the gentlemen to do the same, though Sir Simon's languid movements were almost an insult.

"Certainly, my dear. I daresay that is what has caused you to speak so precipitously," said Miss Cobb, rising also.

But Sincerity was in no mood to placate anyone's feelings, and she looked pointedly at Sir Simon and responded frostily, "No, it was not the headache. Good night, Lizzie, gentlemen."

Miss Cobb bundled her away, pausing only a few seconds to make their excuses to Lady Rutherford. When she would have scolded, Sincerity put up one hand, shaking her head, which had suddenly begun to ache abominably.

Neither spoke on the ride home. They even climbed the stairs in silence, saying only a brief good night before going to their own bedchambers.

Twenty minutes later, dressed in her nightclothes and a large white mobcap, Miss Cobb peeked into Sincerity's room. All was quiet, and she closed the door again. Her stomach rumbled loudly, and she started down the back stairs that led directly to the kitchens.

She poked up the fire and put a kettle of water on to boil. Then she entered the larder, searching for something to eat. Finding a jar of strawberry preserves and a cloth bag with some leftover scones, she trudged happily back to the kitchen table to spread out her feast.

"I thought we had mice," said Crispin, standing in the doorway, still dressed very properly, though he had loosened his cravat.

Flustered, Miss Cobb dropped the knife she was holding.

"You startled me!" she protested.

"I'm sorry, Miss Cobb. I thought you must have heard me come in. I was just locking up for the night," he added, passing behind her and going to the outside door to put on the latch.

"There we are. Do you need anything else, Miss Cobb? Shall I make the tea?"

"I can manage, thank you, Mr. Crispin," she replied, blushing from head to toe as he stood there, and here was she in her nightrail! "You may go to bed," she added, her color deepening.

"I wasn't heading for bed yet. I usually come in here—where it's nice and cozy—and have a cup of tea with a dash of brandy in it before bed. If I'm not too tired, I read a little while," he said, pulling from his pocket a slender book.

Intrigued, Miss Cobb forgot her embarrassment and sat down. "Is that poetry?"

"Yes, but it's not your French poet. This is Byron. I know it's supposed to be romantic drivel, but I quite like it."

"Do you really? I don't know much of Byron's work. He is such a controversial fellow, Lady Hartford didn't want her girls becoming intrigued by him, so she never allowed any of his work in the house."

"A shame," said the butler, pouring two cups of tea.
To one, he poured a dollop of brandy. "Some for you,
Miss Cobb?"

"Just a little. I'm afraid I drank quite a bit of champagne at the card party," she said, wishing the words
unspoken as she watched the mask of polite disinterest
fall into place on his visage. She had chosen the worst
thing to say, reminding him of the gap between them.
Though she was a mere companion, she came from the
gentry. Mr. Crispin was a good man, but he had always
been and would always be, a servant. The two classes
moved in parallel lines; they almost never crossed.

Almost never, thought Miss Cobb. She reached for her
cup, touching his hand as he added several drops of
brandy to it. Their eyes met and held. With a fleeting
smile, Crispin cleared his throat and put away the flask.

"Would you like for me to read you my favorite?"
asked the butler, picking up the book. Her stomach gave
a great growl, and they laughed, the tension eased.

"Yes, do read one, please," said Miss Cobb, picking
up a scone and splitting it open neatly, placing a spoonful
of strawberry preserves inside it.

*"She walks in beauty, like the night*
*Of cloudless climes and starry skies;*
*And all that's best of dark and bright*
*Meet in her aspect and her eyes:*
*Thus mellowed to that tender light*
*Which heaven to gaudy day denies."*

He paused, but Miss Cobb was lost in the words, her
eyes closed in pleasure. He continued with the second
verse and then the third.

*"And on that cheek, and o'er that brow,*
*So soft, so calm, yet eloquent,*
*The smiles that win, the tints that glow,*
*But tell of days in goodness spent,*
*A mind at peace with all below,*

*A heart whose love is innocent!"*

The silence dragged Miss Cobb back to the present. Her nondescript eyes shone with tears, and Crispin closed the book, his hand stealing across the worn kitchen table to take hers.

"I should not speak of this; I know you . . . ," he began, but she shook her head, and he fell silent again.

He disengaged his hand and rose, straightening his coat and saying properly, "I will clear all this away, Miss Cobb. You needn't bother with it."

She was being dismissed, she knew. All she had to do was put her hand on his shoulder. That was all it would take.

"Thank you, Mr. Crispin. Good night."

"Good night, Miss Cobb."

She picked up her candle and climbed the stairs with a heavy tread. When she entered her room, she walked to the full-length cheval glass, holding the candle aloft and studying her face. She didn't notice the door to the sitting room was ajar or see Sincerity watching her, puzzled.

Miss Cobb smiled at her image. Studying it objectively, she turned her face to one side and then the other. There were tiny lines beginning to appear at the corners of each eye. Her skin was still smooth and even, but it wouldn't be long before the years changed all that. She thought about Lady Rutherford's skin that seemed to be too big for her features, sagging about her jaw and neck. She put the candle on a table and patted her neck and chin. Everything was still quite firm.

But what would she look like in ten years? Or twenty? She knew she would not improve with time. And who would care? she asked herself. It really didn't matter. She was meant to be what she was meant to be. Nothing more.

So why were the tears streaming down her cheeks for

the life she had never had, the lost love she had never expected to find in the first place? Blowing out the candle, Letitia Cobb climbed into bed and cried herself to sleep.

Sincerity crept back to her own bed. Her stomach also grumbled its protest, but there was nothing she could do about that. She couldn't very well go back down to the kitchen with Mr. Crispin still about. He might guess that she had overheard their exchange. He might tell Miss Cobb, and if there was one thing she didn't want, it was to make dear Cobbie more miserable than she already was. Miss Cobb had always said no one liked to be pitied.

Besides, maybe Miss Cobb didn't need her pity. Perhaps what she needed was her help, thought Sincerity, a gleam appearing in her eyes as her mind began to turn over one scheme after another.

Why shouldn't Miss Cobb and Mr. Crispin marry? He might not be of the same class, but Miss Cobb's father was only a vicar—never mind that her grandfather had been a baronet or something. That wasn't so far removed. Besides, Crispin was a man of great sense and learning. He was absolutely perfect for Cobbie. Much better than the stodgy Mr. Boynton!

Well, that was all there was to it, decided Sincerity. They belonged together, and since they were both being so silly about it, she would just have to take a hand in matters . . . whether they liked it or not!

With a grimace, Sincerity kicked at the covers. At least it would give her something to occupy her time and her mind besides that Sir Simon McKendrick!

# NINE

On Wednesday, Sir Simon joined friends for a picnic in the country. Except for Miss Lang, the ladies rode in carriages while most of the gentlemen were on horse-back. Peter Jackson, who had wheedled permission for Lizzie Montfort to accompany them, drove his curricle with his prize by his side.

Simon began to feel like a prize himself; everywhere he turned, there was Miss Lang. He could not say two words to anyone without her trilling a laugh or inserting a comment. He didn't think he had given her so much encouragement, but he must have done, he decided dismally. Otherwise, she would surely have understood his brief responses meant that he was not interested in furthering their acquaintance. He hated to be unkind, but he was on the brink of giving her a sharp set-down.

"Why so happy, Simon?" asked Philip Farguson, catching Simon's attention when Miss Lang strolled away for a few seconds.

"Save me, Philip. I think I am well and truly caught. I know I said I was going to remain in Bath through June, but I don't think I can. Miss Lang has become a problem," he replied, looking over his shoulder for his captor.

Nodding knowingly, Philip gave a mirthless laugh. "Can't say as I blame you, old man. I would like to tell you it's all in your head, but I think her mind's set on you and no other. You might be wise to turn tail and run."

"I don't like it," said Simon glumly.

"I suppose that's the curse of having not only a pleasing personality and face, but money and land to boot," quipped Farguson cheerfully. "At least *you* don't have to wait on your father for funds."

"I know. It goes with the territory," said Simon, greeting Peter Jackson warmly. With a grin, he added, "Going quite well with Miss Montfort, I see."

"She's a little gem, isn't she? If I were looking for a wife, she would be the front-runner for sure," said the younger man, giving a little wave to the lovely Miss Montfort.

"Not ready to take the plunge?" asked Philip.

"Not anytime soon. I mean, I'm too young to surrender. Unlike our old friend here," he added, nodding to Simon.

"What the deuce do you mean by that? I'm not that old," demanded Simon.

"No, but the word is out, Simon, old friend. I had Lady Rutherford ask me all sorts of questions about you and your situation. I figure she's sizing you up for someone," said Peter.

"I don't know who it could be! You're the one the granddaughter is chasing, not me. And I haven't any intention of asking anybody . . . ," began Simon, pausing when Miss Lang approached them.

"Sir Simon, could you come carve this ham for us? Mr. Haversham is making a muddle of it, and I told everyone you are an absolute genius when it comes to carving," said Miss Lang, coming up to the trio of friends and latching onto Simon's arm possessively.

He gently removed her hand and said abruptly, "I will

be there in a few minutes, Miss Lang. I'm in the middle of a rather important conversation right now."

"Of course, Simon," she said huskily, looking up at him with adoration in her eyes. "I'll be waiting."

"You know, Simon, you could do worse. I understand she's an heiress," said Farguson with a quick intake of breath. "And devil take me, what a beauty!"

"Then let the devil take you, Philip. I'm not going to offer for anyone. And Peter, if Lady Rutherford should ask again about my intentions or my circumstances, feel free to tell her that I'm an incurable gamester who will probably lose my shirt before the year is out!"

Simon stalked over to his horse and mounted, leaving his friends to invent a tale about his sudden indisposition. He just didn't care anymore.

When Simon returned to the White Hart Inn later that afternoon, his mood did not improve when Angus informed him solemnly, "Someone is making inquiries about you, Sir Simon."

"What sort of inquiries? And who is making them?" asked Simon wearily.

"I had it from one of the maids whose sister works for Lady Rutherford. Didn't you go to a card party at her house the other night, sir?"

Simon shook his head, mystified by this sudden interest in him. "So I did, but I don't understand why she would be asking about me. I mean, I've hardly said a word to that granddaughter of hers." He shrugged out of his riding coat and handed it to the servant.

"I understand the girl's a beauty, sir," Angus said casually, brushing at a spot on Simon's coat.

"Bah! The chit is barely out of the schoolroom! Her grandmother is a dotty old fool if she thinks I'll cast my lot there."

"Perhaps, Sir Simon, but someone has started a rumor that you are, that is . . . I want you to understand, sir, I don't believe it for a moment. I mean, I would know, wouldn't I?"

"Angus, you are wandering from the purpose. What is being said about me?"

"It is said that you are secretly betrothed to someone here in Bath and that you are only waiting until the girl is out of mourning before you make it public."

Simon let slip a quiet curse. Then he said in clipped words, "If anyone should ask you, Angus, you are to tell them from me that they are out of their minds."

"As you say, Sir Simon," replied the valet.

*Playing matchmaker is a thankless job,* decided Sincerity, when Miss Cobb once again refused to cooperate. She had carefully engineered a cozy tête-à-tête for her companion and the butler by going to bed almost at sunset, and still they had bungled the opportunity. Instead, Miss Cobb had declared that she, too, was going to make an early night of it.

And Crispin was even worse! After she had told him that Miss Cobb requested that he find her book of poetry and bring it to her in the library where she was relaxing—alone—Crispin had sent Trudy in with the book.

Time after time in the past week, she had arranged private assignations for them—without their knowledge or consent, of course—and time after time, they had wasted the opportunity!

And to make matters worse, Mr. Boynton was haunting the house on Russell Street like an unwanted specter, popping up at all times of the day! He hadn't put in an appearance yet that day, but he had promised them he would see them that evening at the assembly.

Sincerity was beginning to despair.

"The morning post has arrived, miss," said the butler.

"Thank you, Crispin," said Sincerity, sifting through

a gratifying number of invitations before discovering the letter in her mother's slanting hand.

Leaving her breakfast untouched, she hurried to the library. For some reason, privacy seemed to be of the utmost importance for this letter.

Sincerity turned it over in her hands several times before gathering up enough courage to open the envelope. She unfolded the paper inside, closed her eyes for a quick prayer, and then began to read.

"Confound it!" she breathed, letting the letter drop to the floor. She felt for the chair behind her and sank into it, the color draining from her face.

It seemed her world was coming to an end, and all because she had made up that foolish tale about Sir Simon. Her mother still had no clue about her aunt's death, but she was bound and determined to interfere in her daughter's happiness.

She might have known her mother had connections in Bath who would be spying on her! It was probably Lady Humphries. Cobbie had said something about her being related to Lady Rutherford.

Sincerity bent down to retrieve the missive and forced herself to read again each frightful word, her eyes closing when she read the last critical line.

"Ten days," she breathed.

The door opened and Miss Cobb hurried inside. "Crispin tells me you have had a letter from your mother."

"How the deuce . . . Oh, never mind how he knew. Yes, I have, and it's not good, Cobbie. See for yourself," she said, handing the letter to her friend.

" 'I will arrive in ten days to meet your betrothed. If he has been toying with you, your father will deal with him,' " quoted Miss Cobb.

"You needn't have read that bit out loud, Cobbie. I felt sick enough about it without hearing it spoken."

Frowning, Miss Cobb observed, "But you don't have a betrothed."

"I am aware of that," said Sincerity dryly.

"Sincerity, you must think of something! Ten days is not nearly enough time to bring Sir Simon up to scratch!"

Sincerity laughed, but Miss Cobb was not comforted by the humorless sound. She walked to the sideboard and filled two glasses with some sort of liquor; she didn't know exactly what it was, but it really didn't matter.

"Drink this," she commanded, handing one glass to her charge while she downed the other.

"Perhaps you could persuade Sir Simon to wed you," said Miss Cobb after catching her breath.

"And perhaps the sun will not rise tomorrow," replied Sincerity.

"You can't give up now," said Miss Cobb. "Besides, have you forgotten? You're not just a young lady with a handsome dowry. You have a goodly fortune in your own right. Sir Simon may not be as plump in the pocket as he seems. He might jump at the chance to wed an heiress."

Sincerity sat forward, leaning toward Miss Cobb with unaccustomed determination lighting her face. "What you don't understand, Cobbie, what no one seems to understand is, I do not want to wed! Not Sir Simon, not anyone!"

"But Sincerity, surely you are not serious. I mean, when you have had time to grow accustomed to your new status . . ."

"But I don't have that time, Cobbie, because my parents are going to arrive on my doorstep in only ten days . . . make that eight days. The letter was written two days ago. So you see, there is not time for anything!"

"There, there, my dear. Perhaps your father will intercede for you. After all, he is your guardian, just as Mr.

Cooper said, so if he wants to allow you to remain here in Bath . . ."

Miss Cobb fell silent. Both of them knew the futility of hoping that Lord Hartford could withstand the force of his wife's constant nagging. He was good for a few moments, but they had never known him to remain firm against the strength of her overwhelming will.

"I wish we might have had more time. I wish . . . Sincerity, what are you thinking?" asked Miss Cobb, her face alarmed at the gleam growing in her young friend's eyes.

"You know, Cobbie, something you said has given me pause. Perhaps there is a ray of hope."

"Please, Sincerity, do not do anything rash."

Sincerity jumped to her feet and headed for the door. Turning and giving Miss Cobb a wink, she said, "I shan't tell you what my idea is, but we may come about yet."

Miss Cobb followed her up the stairs, watching in dismay as Sincerity stripped off her genteel morning gown, replacing it with the old riding habit.

"Where are you going in that?" she demanded.

"Don't ask, Cobbie. Ah, Trudy! There you are! Go down and tell Sam to fetch old Nate."

"Old Nate?" asked the maid and Miss Cobb in unison.

"Sam will understand," said Sincerity, pulling on her boots.

She hurried to the mirror and pulled the carefully coiled chignon from its pins. After running a comb through the golden curls, she threaded a blue ribbon through her hair.

"Perfect!"

"Sincerity! You look like a veritable child, a hoyden at that!"

"Don't worry, Cobbie, and keep your fingers crossed."

"Sincerity! Sissie, please!"

Whistling, Sincerity strode to the door and turned, an

irrepressible grin on her lips and that familiar twinkle in her eyes.

"Don't worry. I shan't do anything to publicly disgrace us, Cobbie. While I am out, why don't you find Crispin and read some poetry together!" she added saucily before tripping down the stairs and into the garden.

"What's this, Angus?" asked Sir Simon, stumbling from his bed late that same morning and discovering two bouquets of flowers had been delivered while he slept. "Not Miss Lang again. I thought I had made my disinterest rather obvious yesterday."

"I left th' cards on them, sir. One, I believe, is from Miss Lang. Th' other? I couldn't say," said his valet, taking dishes from a large silver tray and arranging them on a small table.

Simon read the first card, shaking his head. "She hopes I am not angry with her," he said, laying that card aside and opening the next small envelope. "The others are from Lady Rutherford, to thank me for helping her bilk her unsuspecting guests at cards the last week."

"It says that?" asked the valet, his scraggly gray brows shooting upward.

"No, she is not that obvious. But she does thank me and hopes we can be partners at the next evening of chance. She says she is thinking of having a gaming night, a daring entertainment, and could I come by and advise her on what the gentlemen like to play."

"Are you going?"

The look Sir Simon gave his man was enough of an answer and the valet grinned, leaving his master to eat his breakfast in peace.

Simon sifted through the mail that had accompanied his breakfast, putting to one side the few invitations he wished to accept. He had promised his sister he would

stay away for two months, but he doubted he could remain much longer. The society in Bath, after all was said
and done, was not so very different from London.

"What do you want me t' do with the flowers, sir?"

"Throw them out if they bother you, Angus. I don't
want you getting sick from being around the blasted
things."

"As to that, I don't think these make me sneeze like
those yellow things."

"Then keep them. If you like them, put them in your
room. I just don't want to see them again," he added.
"I'm going out for the day. I'm not in the mood to put
up with the charade of polite behavior required at the
Pump Room."

"Very good, sir."

"One more thing, Angus, if any other female sends
me so much as a wilted flower, a glass of wine, or even
a note, you are to turn it away without opening it. Understand?"

"I understand, sir," replied the grinning valet with a
snappy salute.

Simon dressed in buckskin breeches and riding boots,
topping his shirt with a comfortable coat that was too
large to be fashionable. He bypassed the cravat Angus
had laid out on the bed and tied a white neckerchief
around his neck instead. It didn't matter what he wore.
He didn't plan to meet anyone he knew.

Simon took the shortest route out of Bath and up to
the cliffs. He passed several of his favorite sites for drawing, returning to the small meadow with its excellent
view of the abbey spire. He hobbled his gelding and
spread a blanket on the ground, setting close at hand his
drawing materials and the lunch the kitchens at the inn
had packed for him.

Picking up a wooden stand and a leather case, he
strolled away from the cliffs until he came to a small

stream. Crossing over this, he set up an easel and opened the case, selecting the paints he would need. He took a pencil and drew the landscape in broad strokes, including in the foreground the rock-strewn stream. Then he pulled out his brushes and began to fill the canvas with the bright, vibrant colors of the summer day.

Hours passed. Stopping to inspect his efforts, Simon grimaced at the water in the stream. That had always been his downfall. He could never make the water look alive, and this morning's efforts were no better than before. He picked up the canvas and carried it back to the blanket. Then he set up the easel and turned the painting away from him. He would take a break and then look at it again. Perhaps it would improve with time.

Sitting down on the blanket, Simon opened the small basket of food he had taken with him and began to devour the cold ham and bread. He discovered a few biscuits with currants in the bottom and set them aside for Angus to have later. If there was one food he refused to eat, it was currants.

His luncheon finished, Simon lay back on the blanket and gazed at the light clouds floating over his head. It was a fine day, a wonderful day, and he was glad he had escaped his well-meaning friends and those demanding females. He vowed then and there to escape the next day as well. Perhaps that was the secret to contentment—solitude.

Whether it was the solitude or the contentment, Simon fell into a deep sleep.

"Sir Simon," said Sincerity softly, sitting on top of old Nate and staring down at the sleeping man.

He was looking so handsome in the afternoon light, with his sun-bronzed face and dark gold hair that had escaped its ribbon. Biting her lower lip nervously, she looked down at the ground that seemed miles away. She had hoped to have a private chat with him, but now she wished she had brought her groom along.

"Sir Simon."

When he still didn't stir, Sincerity cleared her throat and repeated his name, this time a little more forcefully. Simon turned on his side, facing away from her, his hair fanning out on the blanket like a horse's mane blowing in the wind.

Sincerity muttered, "Oh, bother."

Reaching down, she patted the old horse's neck and then removed her left foot from the stirrup. She had seen her sister kick it free, but she was afraid such a move would startle the old gelding and make him bolt. She unhooked her right knee from where it was securely set, and sat perched on top of old Nate, too afraid to make the leap but too wobbly to remain where she was.

The next move was Nate's, and he swung his head around as if to ask what was taking her so long. Sincerity grabbed at the pommel, but she lost her balance.

"Aiiieeee!" she yelled, sliding down the side of the horse. Her feet hit the ground with a thud, and she stumbled forward, her efforts to catch herself only prolonging the inevitable. Finally she landed. . . .

"What the devil!" shouted Simon, sitting up at her scream and then finding himself thrown back against the blanket as she careened into him, plunging into his chest and knocking the wind out of him.

"Oh, my! Oh, no! Are you all right?" she demanded, scrambling off his chest and pulling him upright again.

Like a fish out of water, Simon's lips moved but no sound was emitted.

"I have killed you!" exclaimed Sincerity dramatically. Simon shook his head, beating at his chest.

"At the very least, I have done you an injury! How can you ever forgive me?" she demanded, her hands groping his chest when she received only a wheezing gasp in reply.

"Water, you need water! Or brandy!" she said, grabbing the discarded basket and tossing out the discarded napkins, the empty bottle of ale, and the carefully wrapped biscuits.

Sincerity continued to dig until strong hands grasped her wrists, stilling her panicked movements and turning her to face her victim.

"I'm fine," Simon managed to say, his words rasping but intelligible.

"Are you sure?" she asked, frowning and searching his face with those big blue eyes. He nodded, and tears sprang to her eyes, spilling over the rims and streaming down her cheeks. She turned her back to him, but he could see her shoulders shaking.

His voice almost normal again, Simon said kindly, "There, there, Miss Hartford. I told you I was fine, or are you crying because you did not manage to, I believe you said, kill me?"

Sincerity whirled around, frowning fiercely, but the laughter in his eyes brought an answering smile to her lips. She hiccuped and giggled.

"That's better," he said, producing his handkerchief and holding it up to her nose. "Now blow."

She took the handkerchief and dried her tears before blowing her nose and saying, "I am so sorry, Sir Simon. I was trying to dismount."

"A novel approach," he said, picking up the smashed biscuits.

"Oh, dear, I've ruined your luncheon."

"Not at all. I wouldn't eat these on a bet. I was going to take them back to my valet. He likes currants. Me, I can't stand them."

"Tell your valet I will make him some more," said Sincerity.

Simon laughed, shaking his head. "You are a most extraordinary young lady, Miss Hartford, to be concerned for a servant, especially one you have never met."

Sincerity sat back on her heels, kneeling before him, her tears once again surfacing. But she was determined not to use tears to persuade Sir Simon to help her.

He touched her chin, lifting it so that he could look into her eyes once more. Quickly, he withdrew his hand, getting to his feet and walking a few paces away before he turned to study her dispassionately.

She was dressed in the old habit again, but today she didn't even wear a hat. Her long curls were loose, flowing down her back with only a thin blue ribbon keeping them off her face. She presented an angelic appearance, but he had reason to be leery of young ladies, even those whose artlessness seemed undeniable.

"Where is your groom today, Miss Hartford?"

"I dismissed him when we made it up to the cliffs," she responded, meeting his gaze boldly.

"That wasn't very wise. How did you expect to dismount?"

"I had hoped you would help, but you were asleep," explained Sincerity, seeing the suspicion leap into his gray eyes. She made a moue and continued. "I called your name three times, but you didn't stir a bit. I was afraid to shout for fear of startling my horse. So I freed myself from the sidesaddle, but I was so high up, I was afraid to move."

"So you decided to leap on top of me to awaken me?" he demanded coolly.

"Really, Sir Simon, you are taking this all wrong. Nate moved, and I slipped. Fortunately for me, you were there to break my fall before I broke my neck."

"I suppose it would be too ungallant of me to say that I find that particular circumstance unfortunate," he commented, but his sense of humor softened the words.

Sincerity couldn't hide her grin at this witticism. "Then may I say how glad I am that you are being gallant, kind sir."

Recalling her purpose, Sincerity clambered to her feet and strolled around the blanket until she was on the far side. She gave her head a little shake and squared her shoulders. Still, the tale would not come.

Simon watched her warily, wishing there was some logical explanation for her being on the cliffs that did not include trying to catch him in the parson's mousetrap. He wasn't a vain man, but there could be no other reason.

Finally, when she still didn't speak, he inquired politely, "Was there some particular reason why you sought me out this afternoon, Miss Hartford?"

"I suppose I had best just come out with it. That's the best way to handle an unpleasant chore, isn't it?"

"You intrigue me, Miss Hartford," said Sir Simon, but he didn't trust her enough to step closer to her.

"Very well. I will try to explain, but I beg of you, Sir Simon, allow me to finish before you answer me."

"I will hear you out, Miss Hartford."

"My mother is coming to Bath," she began.

"How delightful for you both," he said before she frowned him into silence once again.

"No, sir, it is not delightful. My mother's name is Divinity, but let me assure you, she is anything but divine."

"Rather takes after her daughter Sincerity," commented Sir Simon.

"How droll you are, Sir Simon. I never realized. Perhaps I should just leave you now and return to Bath." Sincerity turned on her heel and headed for the path leading back to town. Sir Simon watched her go, allowing her to get out of sight before he started after her.

"Please, Miss Hartford," he said, "won't you forgive me. I said I would listen without comment, and I didn't keep my word. I beg your pardon." She gazed up at him for a second before taking his hand and allowing him to lead her back to the blanket. "Won't you be seated?" he asked graciously.

"Thank you," she replied.

Simon sat down beside her and waited.

"I am twenty-three years old, Sir Simon. I have suffered through four-and-a-half Seasons in London."

"You are intrepid," he said before putting his hand to his lips and making the gesture of locking them.

"My mother decreed that I would accept the next suitor who asked for my hand. When I did not, I was banished to Folkestone. This would not have been so bad, but my mother's continued badgering was impossible to bear."

Simon raised his hand like a schoolboy begging for permission to speak. She nodded, and he asked, "How many offers did you turn down?"

"Oh, I don't remember. There were two, no, three this Season, but I didn't count the first one because he has asked for my hand so many times I neglect to include him. But that is really neither here nor there. What matters is that I do not wish to marry."

Simon could not prevent his snort of disbelief, but he managed to refrain from speaking.

Sincerity expelled a long sigh of exasperation. "I know that every one of my sex is supposed to spend every waking hour planning for and hoping for the proper husband. I know this, but I tell you plainly, I neither want nor need a husband."

"If you are being truthful with yourself, Miss Hartford, you are an extraordinary lady, indeed."

"Let me ask you something, Sir Simon, though you needn't bother to answer. I happen to know that you are a widower. When you decided to come up to the cliffs today, did you have to tell anyone where you were going? When you decided to visit Bath, did you have to time your visit for anyone else's satisfaction? And when you went away to be a soldier, did you ask anyone for permission?"

"Well, when a man marries, he naturally consults his wife before making certain decisions."

"I understand, but if your wife voiced her objections, and you didn't agree with her, did you not do as you pleased?"

"Really, Miss Hartford, my wife passed away years ago," he said stiffly.

"You misunderstand, Sir Simon. I am speaking in generalities. I told you I didn't expect a response. I am sure there are many ladies and gentlemen, too, who are happy in their marriages. But for me, it is not something I choose to do, and now that I have inherited my great-aunt's estate, I have the means to live independently."

"Then why are you so concerned about your mother's arrival?"

"Because my father, and therefore my mother, still controls the purse strings. They can force me to return to Folkestone or London, wherever it pleases them."

"Would your father force you to wed?"

"I honestly don't know, but I believe he might. My mother is a very forceful person," she said, hanging her head dolefully.

"I see," said Simon, studying the way the sunlight shone upon her hair. He forced his attention to the story at hand, saying, "You still haven't explained why you sought me out today."

"I know. It is so very difficult to admit this last to you. I assure you I didn't mean to tangle you up in my web of deceit."

She placed her hand on his arm. Her touch was gentle and warm. He took a deep breath and could smell the lavender of her perfume.

"In trying to reassure my mother that I was still searching

for a husband, I described a man, telling her that I thought he might be the one to take me to the altar."

Simon swore he heard the death knell sound in his ears.

"I'm afraid my description was a little too precise. I don't know how, but I think she figured out who it was. . . ."

"But surely you made up the man, the description. . . ."

"I did embellish on it," she said, looking into his eyes again. "Unfortunately, I used you as the model."

Simon leaped to his feet, a curse slipping from his lips unchecked. He began to gather up the strewn napkins, grabbing at the blanket where she still kneeled, and then throwing up his hands, willing to abandon it. He removed the hobbles from his horse and folded up the easel, throwing the painting to the ground in his haste. He swung onto the big gelding's back and rode away without uttering another word.

Twenty yards away, he brought the horse to a jolting stop. His anger still boiled beneath the surface, but he couldn't leave her like this—alone and frightened and probably unable to mount that old hack of hers.

Twisting in the saddle, he studied her. She hadn't moved. The afternoon sunlight cast a halo on her mendacious head. Sincerity, ha! What a foolish name for a foolish chit!

"Bloody hell," he muttered, turning the horse and riding back to her side.

She looked up at him, her eyes hollow and hopeless. Either she really was a damsel in distress, or she was better than any actress who had ever trod the boards.

Either way, he was a demmed fool.

"What would you have me do, Miss Hartford?"

# TEN

Simon thought he had never seen such a beautiful smile, so full of admiration and humble gratitude. Dismounting, he quietly went about untying the case and easel from the saddle and hobbling his horse again.

When he joined the girl on the blanket, he was dismayed to see tears still flowing from her eyes. Gently, he took the handkerchief from her grasp and wiped them away.

"Now, lass, hadn't you best be telling me what you want me to do before I change my mind?" he asked, smiling.

"Yes, yes, I should. I know you are busy, so I will come straight to the point," said Sincerity, but she had a sudden attack of nerves and floundered. His patience gave her courage, and she began, "I was hoping you would agree to act the part of my suitor while my parents are here."

His shock was tangible, but he didn't run away, and she continued, "I know it is a brazen thing to ask, but their stay should be brief. After they leave, I will write to them and say we decided we wouldn't suit. They will blame me, of course, but they will be occupied with other things by then."

"But from what you have told me of your mother, will

she not then demand you settle on someone else? Surely
you will only be postponing your mother's anger."

"True, but that need not concern you, Sir Simon."

"Very well. Then what shall I do?"

"Well, I think first we should become better acquainted. My mother is not a fool. You should know more
about me, and I should know more about you. I'm afraid
it would mean spending some time together, rather like
school," she said, looking up at him.

"I believe you will find me an apt pupil, Miss Hartford," replied Simon, making himself comfortable, re-
clining on the blanket and propping himself up on one
elbow. "I hope you are equally clever. Now, let's begin.
How old are you? Where were you born? Do you have
any brothers or sisters? If so, how old are they? Come,
come. Surely these questions are not too difficult," he
teased.

Sincerity giggled. "I never would have guessed you
possessed such a sense of humor, Sir Simon."

"Most people do not know it. As a matter of fact, I
make it a practice to be as grumpy as possible. One is
much less inclined to be troubled with friends and such."

"As to that, I am well aware you have several friends
who are very much your champion, not to mention Miss
Cobb, who was quite taken with you."

"Ah, now you are flattering me. But never mind that,
you are trying to evade my questions. I know every ploy
of the schoolboy who has not studied his lessons."

"Why? Because you were one of those schoolboys?"
she asked, her blue eyes twinkling with laughter.

"You have guessed my darkest secret!" he declared,
raising his hand to his brow in a dramatic gesture. "Well,
I suppose I must marry you now."

The twinkle vanished from Sincerity's eyes. His dec-
laration, as theatrical as it was, reminded her powerfully
of her daydreams. She dropped her gaze, unable to meet

his kind gray eyes. The silence between them grew until he touched her hand, giving it a reassuring squeeze.

"It was only a bit of nonsense, Miss Hartford. I didn't mean to make you uncomfortable."

"I know," she managed.

"But you must know that in this masquerade we are embarking upon, there will be times when we must speak untruths, even in our, uh, rehearsals."

"Yes, I do know that, but your words took me by surprise. I really didn't think you would agree in the first place, and I certainly hadn't considered how it would be to have you . . ."

Mistaking her meaning, Simon said, "But you are the same young lady who declared she has no intention of marrying—ever—are you not?" She nodded vigorously. "Then we must try to remember during the coming days that this is all playacting with each of us performing a part."

"You're right, of course. Thank you, Sir Simon."

"Very well. Then we must begin. But first, you must call me Simon." He held up a hand to silence her when she looked ready to protest. "While a couple might not use their Christian names in a real betrothal, I think it would lend credibility to ours."

Sincerity grinned suddenly and nodded. "Done, Simon! And I am Sincerity."

"Very well, Sincerity. But what makes you grin so?"

"I was just thinking how very much my mother will disapprove of the fact that you and I address each other in such a familiar manner. How very delicious that is!"

"Knowing your mother, one might almost say it is divine," said Simon with a wicked laugh that sent Sincerity into the whoops.

After several moments, they began to rehearse in earnest. Sincerity answered each of his questions, but she couldn't bring herself to interrogate him on such intimate topics as his family and home, sticking to subjects like his military career and his schooling.

"I suppose I should be going home now," said Sincerity finally.

"Yes, we've been at it for almost two hours now," agreed Simon, rising and holding out both hands for Sincerity to grasp them and pull up. Her muscles had grown stiff, and she had to cling to him for support for a moment.

"I'm so sorry," she said, that old timidity surfacing once again.

"No need for that. If I weren't so vain, I would have groaned out loud when I stood up just then, but I didn't want you to think you've saddled yourself with an old man," he said with another of those charming laughs that Sincerity found impossible to resist.

She grimaced and nodded toward the horses. "Speaking of saddles, I suppose I have to ride home?"

"It would be the easiest way," he said. "I'll help you up, and if you like, I'll go first. That way, you won't have to look down the steep hills and you needn't worry about your old hack bolting for the barn."

"Thank you, but don't forget to look back occasionally," said Sincerity as he was lifting her into the saddle. "It's not just a runaway horse that frightens me. It's also the possibility of falling off for absolutely no reason. I promise you, I am a terrible horsewoman."

"Why is that?" he asked, swinging up on Soldier and looking down at her as she shrugged her slender shoulders.

They rode abreast for a while until the incline grew steeper and the path narrowed. Simon continued to converse, looking back frequently, as promised.

"You were reared on a country estate. I would think learning to ride would naturally have been part of your lessons."

"Well, I'm afraid the governess we had before Miss Cobb was very nearsighted. Tranquility and I are not identical, but we resemble each other closely enough that she could ride and then tell Miss Russell that it had been me. I didn't mind since I was terrified of falling, and Tranquility loved the extra time on horseback."

Simon chuckled, shaking his head. "Did you pull such pranks often?"

"Only when Tranquility wanted to. I usually just did whatever she told me to." Sincerity ducked her head when he pulled back on the reins and halted their progress.

Simon twisted slowly in the saddle and gaped at her, cocking his head to one side in disbelief. "I hope you will not be offended, Miss Hartford, if I say I find that rather difficult to believe. I mean, given the evidence of what I have seen today, I would say anyone who could cook up this madcap scheme and somehow persuade me, a hardened soldier, to participate in it, could not possibly be the guiltless disciple you describe. Now, admit it, you were right in the middle of those childish pranks, weren't you?"

"I protest, Simon, and I maintain that I am innocent of the charge," replied Sincerity with a wide-eyed gaze.

He turned around, and they continued on their way, but he observed loudly enough for her to hear, "In a pig's eye."

Sincerity giggled, enjoying this friendly badinage. She had never had a gentleman for a friend, and she found trading anecdotes with Simon very stimulating. He was so easy to talk to, she thought, smiling at the back of his head.

They reached the fringes of Bath, and Simon once again rode by her side, a pensive frown on his brow.

"Is something wrong, Simon?"

He stopped both of their mounts and studied her for

a moment before beginning. Sincerity cringed, thinking he had changed his mind, but she said nothing.

"Sincerity, I want to ask you one question before we take this first step by appearing together in public. You will no doubt be offended, but I must ask. But I also want you to know, I will believe your reply, no matter what it is."

"Go on," she whispered, her hands trembling on the reins.

"I spent one Season in London, and most of the people I met there, including—or perhaps especially—the ladies, were devoid of honor and honesty. I was very disillusioned, as you can tell, even after all these years. You may think me vain to ask you this, but I must know if this scheme you have embroiled me in, is it what you say it is? You are not, for instance, trying to trap me into marriage, are you?"

"If I were, it wouldn't work, would it?" she replied honestly.

"No. I would have no compunction about walking away from you and Bath and going home to Scotland. But I hope I am a better judge of character than that."

"You are, Sir Simon. I . . . I must admit that from time to time, I have told a small white lie to cover up a faux pas or a childish transgression, but all that I told you today, from my fear of my mother to not wanting to wed at all, all that is the truth. I give you my solemn word," she said, extending her gloved hand and taking his, giving it a manly shake.

"That's good enough for me," he responded. "Now, my dear Miss Hartford, may I escort you home?"

"You are too kind, Sir Simon," she replied, wondering how he could keep from hearing her heart sing—not from any deeper emotion for the man at her side, she told herself, but from relief over having her dilemma solved on the one hand and admiration for his benevolence on the other.

So at ease were they riding side by side through Bath, that anyone watching the animated couple would have guessed they were old friends, if not more closely connected. By the time they arrived at the house on Russell Street, a schedule for their rehearsals had been agreed upon, and they parted, planning to meet the next afternoon.

Simon dismounted and then helped Sincerity, who slid into his arms without so much as a blush.

"Would you like to come in for a few minutes, Simon?"

"Thank you, but no. I think you should inform Miss Cobb about our little arrangement without my presence. I'll call on you tomorrow at two o'clock as planned," he said, looking down at her. Impulsively, she stood on tiptoe and kissed him on the cheek before tripping merrily into the house.

Simon grinned at Sam who had watched the entire scene with growing interest.

"See that Nate gets a good rubdown," said Simon, flipping a coin to the footman.

"Right you are, guvner," said Sam with a grin.

Simon climbed back into the saddle and turned Soldier for home, whistling as he rode and wondering at the foolish smile on his face. Not only was he still whistling when he entered his rooms, he dropped his case of paints onto the floor, a fact that had his valet observing his master for other signs of idiocy. In all the years that he had served Sir Simon McKendrick, he had never known him to treat his belongings in such a haphazard manner.

"I think I'll join my friends for dinner after all, Angus. Would you mind going down to Farguson's rooms and telling him? Oh, and tell them at the desk to send up hot water for a bath."

"Very good, sir," replied the valet. Simon began stripping off his shirt as he headed into the bedchamber.

Angus had almost made it to the door when Simon poked his head out again and asked, "What did you do with that last bouquet of flowers?"

"I put them in my room, just to get them out of your sight, sir, since they seemed to bother you so."

"How do they look? Are they still fresh?"

"Very. I just didn't have the heart to throw them away."

"Good. Will you see to it they go to Miss Hartford in Russell Street?"

"Miss, uh, Hartford?"

"Yes, I think it's number nine, but I might be wrong. The house belonged to her great-aunt; I forget her name, but you might need to know that when you inquire."

"Very good, Sir Simon," said the valet. "Will there be anything else?"

"Yes, I, uh, want to buy a piece of jewelry. Where is the best place to go?"

"Shall I ask Mr. Farguson when I speak to him, sir?"

"Far . . . No, never mind. I'll ask one of the clerks."

"Very good, sir," said Angus, a smile slowly spreading across his face, adding new folds to his weathered countenance. Humming his own happy tune, he hurried to his room to pick the best bouquet of flowers to send to this Miss Hartford. Whoever she was, he would be happy to make her acquaintance.

Sincerity was both relieved and disappointed when she could not find Miss Cobb. Crispin was also missing, so she couldn't ask him where her companion had gone. She ordered a hot bath, adding a generous measure of lavender to the water to help relax her tired muscles.

As Trudy washed her hair, Sincerity closed her eyes

and began to weave another tale about a hero and heroine. She, of course, was the heroine, and it seemed that Sir Simon McKendrick had taken on the permanent role of hero.

The setting this time was the coast, in a cave where the villain had tied up the heroine to compromise her so that she would be forced to wed him. Enter the hero, Simon. He handily defeated the villain and then turned to untie the heroine—herself—who fell into his arms, weeping, and . . .

Sincerity opened her eyes just as the first pitcher of rinse water cascaded over her head. She closed them tight, rubbing them and whimpering as the soap began to sting and burn.

"I'm so sorry, miss. I thought you saw it coming," said Trudy anxiously. "Let me get you a cloth."

"It's not your fault. I wasn't paying attention. There, that's better," said Sincerity, smiling for her maid's benefit.

"I need to pour some more. Are you ready?" asked the maid.

"Ready," said Sincerity, screwing her eyes shut and returning to the seaside cave in her mind. The hero picked up the heroine, his lips . . .

"Oh, botheration!" said Sincerity.

"Did it get in your eyes again, miss?"

"No, no, I'm fine. Is it all rinsed now? I'm getting cold," she said.

The maid felt one golden strand and it squeaked between her fingers. "All done," she said, turning and picking up the large towel that had been warming by the fire.

In silence, Sincerity dressed in her wrapper and dismissed the maid, sitting by the fire alone and combing her hair until it was dry. Usually, such a solitary undertaking was the time for daydreams, but this time, it was impossible, and she frowned with each stroke of the comb.

It must be Sir Simon, she told herself finally. Now that she was going to become well acquainted with him, he was no longer suitable as the hero for her tales. That had to be it. So Sincerity began to weave her daydream all over again, allowing her fertile imagination free rein. But once again, the hero was not cooperating, and she growled in frustration.

All her life, she had depended on her daydreams to get her through the dull routines of life. Now she couldn't manage a single stimulating mental image. When she closed her eyes, all she could see was Sir Simon looking down at her, taking pity on her, dismounting and returning to her side. But that wasn't a daydream! That was what had actually happened!

A tiny voice she didn't recognize seemed to be trying to whisper some explanation to her, but she couldn't quite hear it.

"Sincerity, did you have a nice ride?" asked Miss Cobb, poking her head in the door, her appearance rather windblown and her hair escaping its pins.

"Actually, yes, I did. I looked for you when I returned, but no one seemed to know where you had gotten to. Or Crispin either, for that matter," said Sincerity, still too taken up with her own concerns to be curious about Miss Cobb's unexplained absence.

"Then perhaps we should ask Mr. Cooper to find us some lady's hacks," said Miss Cobb, handily turning the subject away from her whereabouts. "I would love to go riding with you."

"Oh, I'm hardly ready for a real hack yet. I think, though, that old Nate and I are going to get along all right. I still don't trust him, of course, but I am trying to give him the benefit of the doubt," said Sincerity, her nerves racing as she came to the point of confession.

She moved to the satin-covered sofa and patted the spot by her side.

"I need to speak to you about a matter of some importance, Cobbie, and I don't want anyone to overhear."

Miss Cobb looked ready to bolt, but she walked forward and sat down, folding her hands in her lap and keeping her back ramrod straight. Sincerity didn't notice because she was too busy tracing the rose patterns in the carpet with her bare toes.

"I have done something . . . ," they began in unison.

Exchanging surprised looks, they began to giggle. Perhaps it was only the relief of tension, but their laughter outstripped the humor of their situation, and it was several moments before Sincerity attempted to speak again.

"I know you will not approve, Cobbie, but I went to Sir Simon. . . ."

"And asked him to marry you?" breathed Miss Cobb, her eyes wide and hopeful.

Sincerity giggled again. "In a manner of speaking, but not the way that you advised, Cobbie. I asked him if he would be willing to pretend, and he said yes."

"So you and Sir Simon are going to pretend to wed? I don't know where you will find a clergyman willing to perjure himself. To do such a dishonest thing would mean transportation to some far-off land for him!"

"No, Cobbie, we are not going to pretend to wed, simply to pretend that we are betrothed. Then after a month or two, I will write to my mother and say we decided we would not suit, or some such excuse. That will buy us a little more time. The closer I am to my twenty-fifth birthday when they discover the truth about all this," she said, waving a hand to indicate her meaning, "the more likely it is that Papa will allow me to stay here on my own."

"Oh, I hope it works, Sincerity. I know we have only been in Bath about a fortnight, but I love it here. Perhaps it is because I have grown lazy. You require so little of me, I feel like an equal instead of a paid companion."

Sincerity threw her arms around her friend's neck, giving her a fierce hug. Sitting back, Miss Cobb pulled her handkerchief out of her sleeve and dabbed at the sudden tears.

"You know, Cobbie, I meant it when I said whatever I have is yours. But we should get back to the task at hand before we congratulate ourselves on our good fortune yet."

"Yes, yes, you're right, of course. Back to Sir Simon, the dear man. Why do you suppose he agreed?"

"I can't be sure, but I think the truth of the matter is, he is a gentleman of the first order. When he saw how very distressed I was, he agreed to help. I have never known a man to be so strong and understanding."

"Your papa is understanding," said Miss Cobb, who held Lord Hartford in great respect.

"Yes, but Papa is not strong in his resolve. Anyway, Sir Simon has agreed to spend time with me in the coming week so that we can be as convincing as possible."

"But what will people think? Won't there be gossip?"

"Do you know, Cobbie, I think Simon doesn't really care about what others think. He is willing to play this pivotal role in our little charade, and he only asked one thing of me."

"What was that?"

"He asked if I was telling the truth. And when I vowed that I was, he believed me," said Sincerity, wonder in her voice.

"You sound almost smitten with him," observed the older woman.

Sincerity bristled and shook her head. "Please refrain from making such absurd assertions, Cobbie. I am just amazed that Simon is being so accommodating, and we will have enough to do to make our story plausible without such silliness!"

"Very well, I apologize. Pray continue."

"There will not be an announcement in the papers, of course, but if other people make the assumption that Simon is courting me, then so be it. I got the feeling from speaking to him, that he would welcome people making that assumption. Just between you and me, I think he is being made uncomfortable by someone pursuing him too, shall we say, enthusiastically."

"Really!"

"Yes, I suspect it is that red-haired girl, but needless to say, I didn't ask."

"There is one flaw to your plan, Sincerity. Have you thought what your parents will say when they realize your great-aunt has died? Not only that she is gone, but that you have been deceiving them all this time?"

Sincerity smiled and nodded. "As a matter of fact, I have considered that aspect. Of course they will have to find out later, but for now, Aunt Pru is going to write to her niece about having to go out of town to visit a sick friend."

"Sincerity!"

"Furthermore, she will tell my mother that while she is sorry to miss her, she is glad they will be staying for a few days to act as my chaperon."

"Sincerity, you will never get away with it!"

"Of course I will. I disguise my handwriting. Mother will never suspect, unless Aunt Prudence should write to her from the grave."

"Do not blaspheme, Sincerity," said Miss Cobb, the vicar's daughter.

Sincerity hid her amusement and apologized for her indelicate way of putting things. "But you can see how such a thing might happen. Aunt Prudence has made no secret of the fact that she didn't care for any of her relatives. It would have been just like her to find someplace to go after receiving a letter from my mother saying she was coming for a visit."

"True, but have you thought about the servants?"

"I know, I know. I will have to let Crispin in on the whole thing, and I am not looking forward to that. The others, I think, would be happy to help me. And though I know Crispin has mellowed toward us being here, he is so very strict and honest. I daresay he may cut up stiff. He might even go to Mr. Cooper," said Sincerity, biting at her lower lip.

Miss Cobb patted her hand and smiled. "You just leave Mr. Crispin to me. I believe I will be able to persuade him to go along with our little theatrical production."

"You're a dear!" declared Sincerity, brightening again.

"Why don't you ring for Trudy and dress for supper. I'll go and speak to Mr. Crispin so that we can be comfortable again."

"Thank you, Cobbie."

Letitia Cobb went to her room first and removed the pins from her hair, brushing it out before once again winding it into a knot on top of her head. She pinched her cheeks and bit at her lips before smiling at her reflection and hurrying out the door. She didn't hesitate as she made her way to the ground floor and paused for only a second before knocking on the closed door to Mr. Crispin's sitting room.

"Enter," called the butler who was straightening his collar when Miss Cobb opened the door. "Letitia!"

She stepped over the threshold and closed the door. "Charles, I must speak to you."

He took her hand and pulled her forward, his eyes never leaving her face. She went willingly, her free hand coming to rest against his chest.

"Did you reconsider my proposal?" he asked softly.

"No, not yet. This is of a more delicate nature. I hope

you will not despise me when I have told you what I have to say."

Miss Cobb's knees buckled, and she grasped his hand tightly. He helped her to the closest chair and sat down on the footstool in front of her, keeping her hand in his.

"Nothing you say could make me despise you, my dear. Only tell me what it is."

"Next week, Lord and Lady Hartford are going to come for a visit." Miss Cobb looked down at him with tears in her eyes.

"That is not so despicable, surely," he said with a laugh.

"Sincerity—or rather, *we* have deceived you about the circumstances of her being here."

"But Mr. Cooper has certified Miss Hartford as the true heir," said Crispin, frowning. "Unless she is an impostor!" He relinquished her hands and would have risen, but Miss Cobb grabbed his sleeve.

"No, nothing like that! Please, Charles, it is nothing as bad as that!"

He was not proof against her pleading tone, and he lowered himself onto the stool again.

"Allow me to explain," she added, gratified that he once again held her hands in his. "The Hartfords do not know that Miss Granville has passed. They think Sincerity and I were invited here for a visit by her."

"How in the deuce did they get that idea?" he demanded.

"She wrote to her mother, pretending to be Miss Granville."

"This is intolerable, Miss Cobb," said the butler, extracting his hands from hers and rising. "I cannot be a party to such a scheme, nor can I believe you allowed yourself to be a part of it. What were you thinking? She is, after all, in your charge. Did you not consider that you were deceiving her parents, her rightful guardians?"

Miss Cobb straightened her spine and glared at him. "First of all, I did not know all of this until just before we arrived. But I will tell you truthfully, Mr. Crispin, even if she had told me earlier, I would have endorsed her plan. I would do almost anything for Sincerity Hartford, and unless you can accept that, we cannot continue our friendship."

She paused for breath, and when he didn't respond, she rose and walked toward the door.

"Letitia, wait."

She turned to face him but didn't retrace her steps. For a butler who was adept at hiding his thoughts, Charles Crispin's face was a tableau of conflicting emotions. Miss Cobb sympathized with him; hadn't she felt the same way? But what could she do? Her loyalty lay with Sincerity, not her parents. She would do all she could to ensure that Sincerity would never again be placed under her mother's thumb. And this, perhaps, was the best opportunity. Perhaps Sir Simon was the man to change Sincerity's opinion of marriage and men.

"What do I need to do?" he asked finally, answering her smile with one of his own.

Miss Cobb returned to her chair, and he sat on the stool before her, this time keeping his hands to himself, but he was with her, nonetheless.

"Sincerity Hartford is not the elegant, worldly young lady everyone thinks she is. Did you know she doesn't want to wed?"

"Perhaps she is more like her great-aunt than anyone suspects," observed the butler.

"I only met Miss Granville once, but I believe she might approve of Sincerity's efforts to live her life the way she wants to. And always remember, Charles, Sincerity is the rightful heir to this property. All she really wants to do is live peacefully until her twenty-fifth birthday when she will have control of her estate."

He nodded thoughtfully. "And what will we do when her parents request to see Miss Granville?"

Miss Cobb smiled at his use of the term "we," and she reached out to tenderly stroke his cheek. He grasped her hand and kissed her palm, sending delicious tremors up her arm and into her heart.

She forced herself to return to the challenge at hand and said sensibly, "Sincerity will send a letter to her mother, purportedly from Miss Granville, saying that she has been called out of town for a few days, and she is sorry to miss their visit, and so on."

"How convenient that Miss Granville is not here to defend herself," he commented.

"Lady Hartford and her aunt didn't really get on very well, so it would not be that unusual for Miss Granville to avoid her. After all, have you ever known Lady Hartford to pay a visit to her aunt?"

"Not since I came to serve her fifteen years ago. It just might work."

"Oh, I think it will. The fact is, Lady Hartford will be relieved."

"And his lordship?" asked the butler.

"Lord Hartford will not think anything of it if his wife is satisfied by the tale."

"Very well. Then we shall take steps to inform all the servants about this. I don't think they will quibble about it; I only hope my consequence doesn't suffer from it. When in authority, one must be careful to behave in a manner above reproach."

Miss Cobb smiled at him, and he forgot about the other servants. "Now, my dear Letitia, have you considered my offer?"

She looked down at her hands entwined once again with his. "I need more time, Charles. After this is all over . . ."

"Then I won't importune you," he replied, rising and

pulling her to her feet. She allowed him to kiss her cheek before putting one hand between them and pushing gently away.

"There is one other matter to divulge, Charles."

"When you call me Charles, how can I deny you anything?"

His lips descended on hers, but Letitia Cobb would not be distracted. She turned her head and received another chaste salute to her cheek.

"Lady Hartford believes her daughter is practically betrothed since arriving in Bath."

Mr. Crispin's supercilious brow rose. "Evidently she is a quick study."

"Yes, well, for her mother to be satisfied and go home to Folkestone, it will be necessary for Sincerity to produce her intended."

"Really, Letitia, I cannot countenance some actor . . ."

"Not an actor, Charles, a gentleman. Sir Simon McKendrick, to be precise."

Mr. Crispin snorted in disbelief and said derisively, "And how does Sir Simon feel about his role in Miss Hartford's little farce?"

"He has agreed to participate wholeheartedly and will be coming by every day to learn his part. Mr. Crispin? Charles!"

Miss Cobb helped him to the chair. Whirling around, she spied a decanter and poured him a large measure of liquor. He gulped it down gratefully, his color returning gradually to his face.

"Are you all right?" she asked, patting his cheek when still he didn't speak.

Finally, he shook his head. Bewildered and stunned, he murmured, "The entire world has gone mad!"

# ELEVEN

"Good afternoon, Miss Hartford," said Sir Simon very properly when he entered the drawing room the next day. "And Miss Cobb, it's good to see you again. How are you today?"

"Quite well, Sir Simon. I wanted to thank you for helping my dear Sincerity out of her predicament."

"I am delighted to be of assistance, Miss Cobb."

"And I want to thank you for the lovely flowers," Sincerity said, directing his attention toward her and the large arrangement of flowers at the far end of the room.

"Beautiful flowers for two beautiful ladies."

"Now you are trying to flatter us. Won't you be seated? You'll join us for some tea, Sir Simon?" asked Sincerity.

"Yes, please," he replied, little lines near his gray eyes appearing as he smiled and joined her on the sofa.

"Cream or sugar?"

"No, thank you," he said with a smile. "One more thing to remember about me."

Sincerity chuckled and nodded. "And if the occasion should arise, you must remember never to offer me a cup without cream."

Miss Cobb smiled indulgently on them as they continued in the same vein, each asking the other for his or her favorites.

Finally, Simon said, "Let me see if I can remember all this. First of all, you'll have cream in your tea but only one teaspoon of sugar. You can't abide coffee, no matter how one doctors it up. You love every kind of fruit, but you only tolerate roast beef. You realize, of course, that not liking roast beef is grounds for questioning your English pedigree."

"Really, Sir Simon, you mustn't tease her so in front of her parents, especially Lady Hartford," advised Miss Cobb.

"Cobbie is right. My mother has no sense of humor."

"I'll try to remember that," he said. "Now, what else is there? Let's see, you love sweets and, for some absurd notion, prefer to sneak your currants while the cook is not looking, instead of having them cooked in anything like biscuits." He shuddered at the idea.

"Most impressive, Sir Simon," said Sincerity, her blue eyes twinkling.

"Thank you. Oh yes, there is one more thing I know about you that you did not divulge yourself. You are an excellent card player even though my friend Philip Farguson is not willing to agree with Miss Cobb's assessment."

"If you refer to the other night, I was distracted, sir."

"A truly dedicated player doesn't allow himself, or herself, to be distracted. Now, let's see how well you remember my likes and dislikes," he said, sitting back with a smug smile.

"If you will excuse me," said Miss Cobb. "I think I have learned enough for one day."

"You're leaving us alone?" asked Sincerity.

"Hardly alone. If I know Crispin, he is busy in the hallway even as we speak. And you two are supposed to be betrothed, you know. There can be nothing so scandalous attached to that."

"I shall try to control my ardor," said Simon, grinning wolfishly at Sincerity, who stuck out her tongue at him.

"As I said, children, I have heard enough for today. Enjoy yourselves."

When they were alone, Simon commented thoughtfully, "I don't know whether to feel insulted or flattered."

"Whatever do you mean?" she asked, her eyes sparkling with laughter. She had already learned what that particular tone of his meant; he was about to make some absurd observation.

"Only that I don't know if it is flattering to think I have won Miss Cobb's trust after such a short acquaintance, or if I should be insulted that she places so much confidence in my ability to act the gentleman. Am I such a dandy that she doesn't think me capable of seducing you?"

Sincerity gurgled with laughter, but she managed a quick-witted response, saying, "I should think it is an insult to me, Simon. Perhaps she knows I am too plain to incite you to such a scurrilous deed as seduction."

"You? Plain? Ah, now you are fishing for compliments. Anyone who has the temerity to accuse you of plainness had best be ready to draw his sword!" he declared, leaping to his feet and assuming his battle stance.

"Would you care for some fresh tea, Miss Hartford?" asked Crispin, appearing suddenly in the doorway.

Simon hurriedly took his seat, winking at Sincerity.

"No, thank you, Crispin." She turned to Simon, grinning as the butler disappeared as suddenly as he had appeared. "Would you care for another biscuit, Sir Simon?"

"Is there a plain one?" asked Simon formally, accepting the proffered sweet. "That's good. Thank you, Sincerity. However, I must remind you to accustom yourself to calling me Simon."

"I am sorry. I forgot about our pact momentarily, but

that would hardly be fatal to our plan. I agreed to that familiarity to add a touch of authenticity to our performance. My mother will probably admonish me for such intimacy, even with my supposed betrothed."

"But an excellent idea, all the same, don't you agree?"

"Yes, I do. Besides, I quite like it when you call me Sincerity," she replied honestly.

Simon McKendrick felt a slight flicker of warmth quicken deep within his soul. He frowned, trying to recall the last time he had experienced such a flutter, however brief. But it was gone, and he shrugged it off, returning to the present and the beautiful girl by his side.

"Then, Sincerity, now it is your turn. What earthshaking facts do you recall about me?"

"First of all, you do not like currants in any form. You prefer coffee to tea, although you usually have it only in the morning, settling for tea whenever you are out. You love any sort of meat or vegetable, but you don't like fruit very much, except apples."

"Very good," he said. "Now, where is my estate?"

"In Scotland, the Galloway district, to be more precise. You raise sheep for wool and also have cattle."

"Excellent. Now, let me tell you about my family. You were very careful yesterday not to pry, but you should know something of my background."

"If you don't mind, Sir . . . I mean, Simon," she said shyly.

"I don't mind. I don't often talk about my family. There are not many of us left. I have an uncle and aunt or two. And now I have a brother-in-law to go along with my sister, Jessica."

"Did she recently wed?" asked Sincerity as if this were the most normal conversation in the world to have with a gentleman who was virtually a stranger to her. But nothing about Simon was normal, she thought, watching the way his lips moved when he spoke, and for some inexplicable reason, he was less a stranger to her than any other man she had ever met.

"Jessie married Robert Selkirk just before I came to Bath. He's a fine fellow, a physician. He lives in Edinburgh, or rather, they live there."

"Is Jessie younger than you?"

"Yes, she's only twenty years old. I missed most of her growing up, since I left for the Peninsula when she was only twelve. My father was still alive then, of course, so it wasn't as if I were leaving her all alone."

"And your father is gone now?" asked Sincerity.

"Yes, he died just before Napoleon surrendered the first time. I didn't make it home, of course. And then, before I could sell out, Napoleon escaped, and it looked like we had it all to do over again."

"Why did you become a soldier, Simon? I have always wondered why any man would leave his home and family, and go off to fight, knowing he might never return."

"It's pride in your country, the need to help others," he said, his tone growing more distant as he spoke. "At least, that is what we tell people when they ask. As for me, it was mostly because I couldn't bear to be at home after my wife died in childbirth. I suppose I was running away."

Sincerity's eyes filled with tears, and she placed her hand over his, not knowing what to say. Simon looked at that delicate hand, so small it scarcely covered his.

"I have never admitted that to anyone before, except myself. You are a good listener, Miss Hartford."

"Sincerity."

The next few days passed swiftly for Sincerity and Sir Simon. He found himself looking forward to their days together, a fact that both amused and confounded his friends.

He came upon a glum-looking Mr. Boynton early one afternoon in the Pump Room. After an initial smile, the large man fell into morose silence again.

"Anything I can do to help, Boynton?" asked Simon.

"Nothing, Sir Simon. My troubles are of a delicate nature."

Mistaking the matter, Simon said cheerfully, "The doctors say these waters can work wonders. Chin up, old boy." Never mind that his new brother-in-law had advised him to avoid taking the waters at all costs.

"No, it's not that. It's something more personal."

"I see. I don't want to pry then. Good day to you, sir."

"Sir Simon, wait. Maybe there is something you can do. I mean, you have entrée into the household where I do not."

"What household?" he asked warily.

"Miss Hartford's house."

Simon stiffened and rose. "I would appreciate it if you would not bandy her name about in a public place, Mr. Boynton."

"I apologize, Sir Simon. I didn't mean to give offense. It is just that I have called twice in the past three days, and each time that starchy butler of theirs refused to take me in to see the ladies. It's as if he is their father and doesn't think I am good enough for her."

Simon knew full well why Boynton was being turned away, but he couldn't very well explain that he and Sincerity were too busy planning their strategy to allow any visitors. After all, wasn't he a visitor himself? He frowned. He certainly didn't feel like a visitor anymore. When he entered that house to spend the day with Sincerity, it was like coming home instead of visiting.

"Excuse me, Sir Simon," said Boynton, loudly enough to wake Sir Simon from his trance.

"What? Oh, sorry. Yes, I have been known to visit,

but you mustn't assume I have any influence over the ladies in the household."

"Perhaps, but may I ask one question. You need only tell me, and I will take the hint." Simon nodded, and Boynton continued, his face red with embarrassment. "Do you go there to see the younger or the elder lady?"

Simon frowned. He had cautioned Boynton about spouting off Sincerity's name in a public place, but he was unsure what the large man was hinting.

"I don't quite understand," he replied, lowering his voice. "Are you asking if I am seeing Miss Hartford or Miss Cobb?"

"That is precisely what I need to know, Sir Simon. I shall step aside, of course, if it is the, uh, elder lady who has caught your attention."

Simon almost laughed. True, Miss Cobb was only five or ten years his senior, but the idea that he might be courting her was too funny. She would laugh, too, he felt sure. Not that he would mention it to her.

"My interest is in the younger occupant of that household, Mr. Boynton. I had no idea your attention had been captured by the other lady. Did this happen after Lady R's card party?"

"The attraction is longstanding, on my part. I am unsure of the lady's interest, even now, when I have so much to offer her."

"So it is that serious," said Simon with a sigh. He really wanted to see Sincerity alone again. There was something he wished to give her, but he sympathized with Boynton's situation. Unrequited love was not a happy state of affairs, and he had the power to have Boynton admitted to the house.

"I tell you what, Boynton. I'll take you around with me. Once we're inside, you will have to convince the lady to see you, but . . ."

"Oh, thank you, Sir Simon. Thank you so much."

"If you'll excuse me for a moment, I need to speak to Mr. Jackson about a matter of importance before we go."

"Certainly," said the big man, who proceeded to dance from one foot to the other in a syncopated rhythm of impatience.

Simon quickly excused himself and led the way to the quiet house on Russell Street. His confident knock went unanswered for several moments. He was a little early, but he had never known Crispin to not be on duty. He knocked again.

"Simon?" asked Sincerity, opening the door wider when she saw him waiting. "Oh, and Mr. Boynton. Won't you come in, gentlemen."

Sincerity looked over her shoulder, but she allowed them to enter. "I don't know where Crispin has gotten to. Won't you come into the drawing room?"

"I was hoping Miss Cobb might be at home," said Mr. Boynton, holding his hat in his hand and twisting its brim nervously.

"I am not certain, Mr. Boynton. Please be seated. I'll see if I can find anyone," she scowled at Simon, and he followed her into the entryway again.

"What's wrong? Doesn't Miss Cobb want to see him?"

"No, she's not been 'at home' to him all week."

"Poor devil. He's got it bad," said Simon, smiling back at the country squire while he spoke.

"Well, Miss Cobb will just have to set him straight—gently, of course. I'll see if I can find her. She has probably fallen asleep reading in the library," said Sincerity, stepping down the hall and opening the door to the library. "Merciful heavens!"

Simon came running; Mr. Boynton came running; Hervé, Sam, and Trudy came running.

"What the devil!" said Simon with a shout of laughter

that he quickly silenced when Sincerity favored him with a cold glare.

"Devil take me!"

"Oh dear!"

"Ah, *l'amour!*"

"Bless me!"

The exclamations sounded like a line of infantrymen firing off their rifles in quick succession.

"Shut the door!" shrieked Miss Cobb, her command making Sincerity spring into action, slamming the door with a resounding boom.

"I am so sorry, Mr. Boynton," she said, pulling at his sleeve to lead him back to the drawing room. She was seconded in this by Simon who took the big man's other arm. When he was seated, Simon poured him a large glass of brandy and thrust it into his hands. He downed it in a single gulp.

"I, uh, I should be going. Please tell Miss Cobb . . ."

The good lady entered the room herself, her skirt now down around her ankles, all the buttons of her bodice fastened, and her hair hastily smoothed into place.

"Sincerity, Simon, please leave us alone for a few minutes."

Sincerity led Simon through the hall to the gardens, her surprise changing to amusement with each step. How could she not have guessed?

"What are you laughing about? Your Miss Cobb was absolutely mortified, and you are laughing," scolded Simon.

Sincerity sat down on the cold stone bench and shook her head, her eyes still twinkling.

"I'm not laughing at her embarrassment, or Crispin's either, for that matter. I'm laughing at my own stupidity, my lack of awareness. I have been so caught up in my own affairs, I haven't even noticed how often Miss Cobb has disappeared without a trace, never telling anyone where she is. At the same time, I have wondered where Crispin had gone. It never occurred to me to put two and two together."

"Well, one doesn't expect a lady of Miss Cobb's modesty to . . ."

"To tie her garters in public?" said Sincerity, completing his thought perfectly.

Then Simon chuckled and said, "Or in the library."

They couldn't keep the laughter at bay any longer. The sight of the very proper Miss Cobb sitting on the starchy butler's lap, hands everywhere and lips firmly locked . . . It was too much for them.

"I am happy to have offered you so much amusement." The haughty tone didn't fool anyone, and Sincerity leaped to her feet and went to her friend, throwing her arms around her neck for a quick hug before pulling her forward to the bench.

"Cobbie, dearest Cobbie, do not think we are laughing at you," she said, but the look on her companion's face caused her to add truthfully, "That is, we were laughing, yes, but it was from the shock at first."

"Miss Cobb, I most humbly apologize to you. We were being a trifle silly; that's all. Please forgive us; forgive me," said Simon. "Now, I'll leave you two alone to sort things out. Sincerity, I'll call for you at four o'clock for our ride," he added with a broad wink. She nodded before shooing him on his way.

Miss Cobb sat down on the bench, wishing the cold stone could cool her shame. Sincerity joined her there. Neither spoke for several moments.

"I have told Mr. Boynton that I cannot ever care for him."

"Was he very upset?"

"Angry would be the best term. I'm afraid I have made an enemy there, but it cannot be helped. No matter what else happens, I would never consider accepting his offer."

"Certainly not if your heart is engaged elsewhere," said Sincerity.

Miss Cobb buried her face in her hands, shaking her head. Finally, she said, "I know you must think it strange and unnatural of me to engage in an activity that I always preached against."

"Perhaps," said Sincerity. "Perhaps not. I am more interested in the why, Cobbie, though you owe me no explanation."

"I don't know how it happened, Sissie. I never thought to find love at my age . . . and a servant!"

"A respected butler," said Sincerity, reaching up and putting a comforting arm around her friend's bony shoulders.

"Yes, but who would ever have thought it could happen like this? I feel like a schoolgirl when I am with Charles. At first, I was very cautious, but then he asked me to be his wife. . . ."

"His wife? But Cobbie, how wonderful!" exclaimed Sincerity, hugging her friend's neck ferociously.

Disengaging herself, Cobbie shook her head. "It isn't that easy, my dear child. What am I to do? If I marry Charles, then I am no longer suitable to serve as your chaperon."

"And if you don't marry him?"

"I will be too miserable to continue."

"Then you will marry him. Goodness me, Cobbie, I can certainly find someone else to lend me consequence. Then we can just go on being friends."

"You make it sound so easy."

"But it is! There is no reason the two of you can't continue to live here. I know!" said Sincerity, clapping her hands with glee. "You and Crispin can have my aunt's old room, the large one that overlooks the street."

"But Sissie, my dear, that should be for the mistress of the house. And if you were to wed . . ."

"We both know that is not going to happen," Sincerity said firmly, her mind already remodeling the large compartment to make it more habitable for the happy couple.

"No, Sissie, I can't," said Miss Cobb, tears streaming down her cheeks.

"Letitia, please," said Mr. Crispin, standing several paces away, his heart in his eyes.

Sincerity rose from the bench, smiling at both of them as she motioned him forward.

"I will leave you two alone to make your decision. But Cobbie, remember, your happiness is of the utmost importance to me. Anything short of that, and I will be gravely disappointed."

Sincerity entered the house through the back door and made her way to the kitchens. She laughed when the other servants scattered from their vantage point by the kitchen windows.

"Well, are they embracing again?" she asked, peering through the thick glass. "I can't tell."

"If *l'amour* has its way," murmured Hervé, wiping a tear from his eye.

"What's this *l'amour* you keep talking about, Mr. Hervé?" asked Trudy.

"*L'amour*, it is love. And with these two, I think love will triumph," said the Frenchman.

"Do you really think so?" asked Sam doubtfully. "Uncle Charles is pretty hard to get along with. I think Miss Cobb might get tired of his ways."

"She'll be able to handle him," said Sincerity with a little laugh. "If she could handle my sister Tranquility, she can handle anyone."

"Sh! Here they come. Go about your business!"

\* \* \*

"They have already gone to see the bishop for the license."

"A special license? That's not inexpensive," said Simon, his attention on Sincerity's seat in the saddle. "Sit up straighter. I know you ladies never let the back of the chair touch your spine. Try to pretend there's an invisible chair behind you that you are trying to avoid touching."

Sincerity made a face at him, but she sat up taller in the saddle, tossing her head so that the curls falling down her back bounced up and down. His mind was trapped by the dazzling sight, and he wondered what she would do if he reached out and touched those curls. Probably slap him and ride away as fast as she could. Considering her fear of horses, that couldn't be too fast, he thought with a sly smile.

"You haven't heard a word I have said, Simon McKendrick."

Simon snapped back to the present. No one had called him by his first and last name in that tone of voice since his mother had passed away. No, that wasn't exactly true. He recalled a few times when Annie had been so angry with him, she had. . . .

"Simon, is something the matter?" she asked, her annoyance changing quickly to concern.

He smiled down at her and shook his head, forcing the memories back to the shadows of his heart.

"No, I was only woolgathering. Now, what were you saying?"

"Mr. Crispin and Miss Cobb want to be married tomorrow morning. The bishop has agreed, but they need two witnesses and have asked us to be there."

"What about Sam and Trudy?"

"They will be helping Hervé prepare the wedding breakfast. Do you agree to be a witness?"

"That depends, Sincerity. Have you spoken to Miss

Cobb? Is she certain she wants to do this? You and Crispin haven't talked her into it, have you?"

"Really, sometimes you treat me like a child!" she exclaimed, urging Nate ahead.

Simon watched her progress, gratified at the confidence she had developed in the past week when riding. He would turn her into a first-rate horsewoman yet!

What was he talking about? Another week, and her parents would be gone. If they weren't able to fool them, then Sincerity would be dragged back to Folkestone with them. If he and Sincerity could convince her parents that they were destined for matrimony, then her mother would be satisfied and would return to Folkestone alone.

And when her parents were gone, there would be no need for him to visit her every day, to ride with her, to dance with her at the assemblies. He could do as he pleased.

A shadow crossed his heart. That was the trouble. Riding across the meadow, laughing with Sincerity, talking to her, listening to her . . . This was all he ever wanted to do.

All of a sudden, it was so clear! He wanted to shout it from the housetop! He loved Sincerity Hartford!

He urged Soldier forward, easily catching up to the plodding Nate. Smiling down at her, he said, "I love you, Sincerity."

She stuck out her tongue at him, a habit she had that made him want to wring her neck at that moment.

"You needn't try to turn me up sweet with your folderol, Sir Simon. I asked you a simple question, and I am still awaiting your answer."

Simon growled, "What was it?"

"Will you come to church with me in the morning and be a witness for Miss Cobb and Mr. Crispin?"

"I will," he replied curtly. Devil take her and all other

women to boot! Here he was, baring his heart to her, and she didn't even have the decency to believe him!

"Let's go back to town. I'm starving," said Sincerity.

"That's fine by me," snapped Simon, quickening the pace until she shouted her displeasure. He slowed Soldier to a walk, but he remained silent the rest of the way home.

"But, Sincerity, I am not a girl, no matter that this is my first wedding!" exclaimed Miss Cobb when she looked at her reflection in the cheval glass. "Trudy, if you do not straighten out these ringlets, I refuse to go to the church!"

"Yes, Miss Cobb! I'll have it back to normal in an instant," said the maid applying the brush to the rejected curls vigorously.

"And I'll have no more of this foolishness, Sincerity. I don't want Mr. Crispin to wonder who is standing up with him."

"Of course not, Cobbie," said Sincerity. "But you must realize that you are looking exceptionally beautiful this morning."

"All brides are beautiful," said the very mature bride, tweaking the lace trim on her gown that had a tendency to roll instead of laying flat. "I shall have to change again."

"Certainly not," declared Sincerity with unusual force. "This is far and away your prettiest gown, and you are not going to change to another. For goodness sake, we should have been downstairs five minutes ago."

"There, Miss Cobb. That does it," said the maid. "You do look a treat, even if I say so myself."

They held their breath while Miss Cobb rose and walked back to the full-length mirror. Her hair, except for two attractive curls on each side of her face, was scraped back in its usual bun, a coiled chignon at the crown of her head. The lace on her gown was finally smooth. She touched the topaz pendant that Sincerity had given her and smiled.

With a nervous gulp of air, she said, "Very nice, Trudy. Thank you for your patience."

"You look beautiful," said Sincerity.

"Thank you. Well, I suppose we are ready to go. Let me think. Have I forgotten anything?"

"Certainly not. No more procrastination. Let's go to church," said Sincerity, stepping behind her friend and propelling her out the door and toward the stairs.

"Really, Sissie, there is no rush. I'm not sure . . ."

"Letitia, you look beautiful, absolutely beautiful," said the butler, waiting anxiously at the foot of the stairs.

Blushing, she put her hand in his, calling over her shoulder as he led her to the front door, "Come along, Sincerity. We don't want to keep the bishop waiting."

Sincerity hurried after them. At the gate, clean and polished, waited Aunt Prudence's old carriage with young Tom standing by the door and Mr. Lorrie on the box, both dressed in formal livery and smiling happily.

She settled onto the wide seat beside Miss Cobb, and Mr. Crispin sat on the opposite side.

"Wouldn't you rather sit beside Miss Cobb?"

"No, thank you, miss," said the butler.

"It's a lovely day," she said, but received no response from her traveling companions who were obviously wrapped in their own thoughts.

Smiling, Sincerity decided to do the same. Drifting into a favorite daydream, she tried her best to lose herself, but it was impossible. She grimaced and stared out the window. Since she had been spending so much time with Simon, she found it impossible to lose herself in her dreamworlds. Drat the man!

The carriage stopped, and the groom threw open the

door. Mr. Crispin descended first, then turned and took his bride's hand to help her out.

"You go on inside," said a deep, smooth voice. Sincerity felt her heart spring to attention, but she held out her hand without speaking, still put out with him for teasing her on their ride the previous day. How could he have been so callous?

"You look very fetching today, Sincerity," he whispered as he escorted her into the church.

She wanted to return the compliment for he was wearing his full Scottish regalia, with his dress kilt and sash and the stockings that stopped below the knees.

"You're staring, little one. Does that mean you have forgiven me for yesterday?" he asked, his breath ruffling her curls.

"Perhaps," she said, glancing up at him and smiling. "I cannot stay angry when you look so very handsome and seem so penitent."

"Perhaps it is being in church, lass, that makes me so contrite."

"And perhaps it is the idea of getting your way," she replied, adding, "Sh! Here comes the bishop."

Twenty minutes later, they were on their way back to Russell Street. Sir Simon and Sincerity facing backward, chatted amicably to each other while the newly married couple held hands and communicated with glances and sighs.

The wedding breakfast was a quiet affair. The groom's niece and nephew were included, and Hervé spent almost as much time in the dining room as he did in his kitchen. Sincerity had insisted that Crispin choose the best wines and champagne from her aunt's cellars, and the food was delicious. Simon offered the first toast and from there, the festivities quickly grew more relaxed and very jolly.

When the last cover had been removed and the fruit-filled wedding cake shared, Mr. Crispin whispered in Miss Cobb's ear. She blushed a rosy color and rose. Making a short speech of thanks, Mr. Crispin led his bride out of the dining room and up the stairs.

Sam and Trudy began to clear the table. Simon rescued the last bottle of champagne and two glasses and led the way to the drawing room. Sincerity smiled shyly at him as she joined him on the sofa.

"You're very quiet, Sincerity. Are you disguised?"

"Disguised from two glasses of champagne and a glass of wine? Certainly not," she said tartly.

"Good, because this is our last day to practice our parts before your parents arrive tomorrow."

She shuddered and begged him not to remind her.

"But you know we should practice as much as possible. I'm afraid your mother may guess we are only playacting."

"Oh, do not say so, Simon. So much has happened since yesterday. I cannot bear to think of being discovered."

"I understand, and I was thinking that our acting needs a little help," he said, pouring two glasses of champagne.

"Help?" she asked, taking the glass he offered her.

"Yes, but first, I want to propose a toast to us," he said, raising his glass.

"To us? I don't think that is necessary."

"There, you see! That is what I mean, Sincerity. Just when I say something loverlike, you draw back. If you do that tomorrow . . ." He left the thought unspoken, but he could see that he had won her over.

"Very well, what is your toast?"

"To the success of our mission."

"To success," she echoed, drinking deeply from the glass. "Take it easy on that," said Simon, taking the glass from her unresisting hand. Sincerity grinned up at him, sighing sleepily.

"There is one other thing we should do that I feel would ensure our success."

"What is that, my dear Simon?" she asked, her words slurring slightly. Sincerity frowned and straightened her spine, breathing slowly and deeply.

"I think we should practice an embrace."

"An embrace? Certainly not!" said Sincerity, sobering rapidly.

"But we may need to take just such a drastic measure at some point, and we will look the veriest fools if we haven't practiced first."

"Well, I suppose you may be right."

"Anything for the masquerade," he murmured, slipping one hand around her shoulder and placing the other on her waist. "Now, put your arms around me."

Sincerity did as she was bid, forgetting all her trepidation as his lips touched hers in a tender kiss.

She drew back and asked suspiciously, "This is just for practice, isn't it?"

"Certainly it is," he lied, guiding her lips back to his.

Simon's efforts paid off when she relaxed against him, clinging to his neck and running her fingers through his hair. He ignored the voice that told him she was intoxicated by the champagne rather than him, and he deepened his kiss. Sincerity moaned, and somehow slipped onto his lap, arching her back as she lay in his embrace, aching for his touch.

Simon left a trail of kisses down her throat, his lips reaching the creamy swell of her breasts. Her hands twined in his hair, she pressed his face against her.

"What is the meaning of this!" shrieked Lady Hartford, slumping against her husband.

Lord Hartford shoved his wife into the closest chair, strode across the room and grabbed his daughter's suitor by the collar. When Simon leaped up, Sincerity fell to the floor with an angry yelp, sounding like a ruffled kitten.

"You must be Sincerity's father," said Simon, extending his hand. His reflexes slowed by the wine and passion, he didn't duck fast enough and went reeling when Lord Hartford's fist connected with his left eye.

"Father, no! You mustn't hurt Simon! Oh, Simon, my dear love!" wailed Sincerity, throwing herself against his chest.

Simon grinned, tried to sit up, and fell over as Sincerity passed out on top of him.

# TWELVE

"Ooooh," moaned Sincerity, trying to sit up only to fall back again, holding her aching head.

"There, there, pet. Don't try to move. I have a drink for . . ."

"Please, nothing to drink," she replied weakly, closing her eyes and turning away. "What time is it?"

"It is seven o'clock," responded Cobbie, then added, "In the evening."

Sincerity sat up slowly and managed to keep the world from spinning around her. "Cobbie, was I dreaming, or did my parents arrive today?"

"Unfortunately, you were not dreaming," said her friend, a wistful note to her voice. "Fortunately, Charles and I overhead the commotion and quickly vacated your aunt's old room."

"But, Cobbie, this is supposed to be your wedding night," whined Sincerity who wasn't quite sure what that entailed, but was quite sure one wouldn't wish to miss it.

Her friend confirmed this with a sensible, "There are other nights, my dear. We will laugh about this one day— all of us. Now drink this down like a good girl."

Sincerity obeyed, making a face as she did. "Oh, I don't think I shall ever laugh again."

"Of course you will. You'll soon start to feel more the

thing. Charles says this concoction of his is wonderful for someone who has been castaway. Now, just lie down and rest. Your mother has gone out this evening, so you may rest easy until morning."

"Where is she?"

"I think she was going to the assembly in the Upper Rooms."

"I hope no one even speaks to her," said Sincerity with a pout. Then in a small voice, she asked, "What about Papa?"

"I believe your mother and father had enjoyed each other's company a little too much on the journey from London. Your father was going to see if he could find some quieter form of entertainment."

"And Simon?"

"Gone back to his rooms to nurse his bruises."

"Bruises," whispered Sincerity, the blurry remembrance beginning to clear. "Oh dear, Papa didn't really hit him, did he?"

"I'm afraid he did. Fortunately, Sir Simon had too much sense to strike your father in return. After making certain you were not injured, he beat a hasty retreat."

"Oh," sighed Sincerity. "Do you think I should send him a message?"

"I think you should go to sleep, pet. You're going to need your rest to face tomorrow."

Sincerity snuggled under the counterpane, looking very much like the young girl Miss Cobb had once tucked in every night. With a fond smile, she leaned over and kissed her charge.

"Good night, Cobbie. I do love you, you know."

"I know. And I love you, too, my little hoyden. Now go to sleep."

When Miss Cobb entered her bedchamber, she found her husband waiting for her. She went straight to his embrace, turning her face up for his kiss.

"Hardly the sort of wedding night I had in mind," he said.

"Me, either, Charles, but there will be many other nights."

"I know. I've put a chair against the door so we shan't be disturbed." He nodded in the direction of Sincerity's room, and continued, "Do you think she'll get away with it?"

"I doubt it, but I couldn't tell her that."

"Well, my love, she won't fail on my account. After meeting Lady Hartford, I'll do everything I can to make certain she never suspects a thing!"

"You're a good man, Mr. Crispin," said his wife.

"Ah, if you only knew, Mrs. Crispin."

"Wake up, young lady! Wake up this instant!"

"Oh, no, please, what is it, Mother? I'm too tired."

"I said wake up," snapped Lady Hartford, holding high a candelabra of lighted candles.

"I'm awake," said Sincerity, sitting up in the bed and trying to force open her eyes.

"Look at me," demanded her mother, setting the candles on the table by the bed. "Look at me and tell me you have not been lying to me for weeks, perhaps months!"

Sincerity frowned, squinting at her mother and shaking her head. She ventured a cautious, "I don't know what you mean."

"I know everything!"

"Everything?" whispered Sincerity who could feel her world, her real world tumbling down around her ears.

"Yes. Lady Rutherford told me Aunt Prudence has been dead and buried for over a month! Now, do you want to explain to me how I received a letter from her stating that she would be visiting a sick friend this week?"

"She wanted to give you the news of her death gradually?"

Lady Hartford responded to this levity by raising her hand and delivering a stinging slap that made Sincerity's teeth rattle. She raised her hand again, and her daughter closed her eyes, but the blow never landed. Sincerity looked up and smiled at her father who held his wife's arm tightly.

"Not again, Divinity."

"You don't know what she did," railed his wife.

"I heard what you said, and I heard Sincerity's flippant rejoinder, but I haven't heard the real reason for her lie." He turned to his daughter and said flatly, "And a very nasty lie it was, young lady. You have jeopardized your good name and Miss Cobb's, also."

"I'm sorry, Papa," she replied remorsefully.

"I'm sure you are, now that you have been caught. But for tonight, we are all exhausted. We will retire and speak of this more in the morning. Good night, puss. Come along, Divinity."

"Hartford, you don't know the half of what has been going on here!" complained Lady Hartford.

"Sh! For goodness sake, Divinity, let the girl sleep tonight. Let all of us get some sleep."

"And that's the whole story, Papa. I discovered that Aunt Prudence had left her estate to me, and I wanted to come to Bath to live. I know I have been a sad disappointment to you, Mother. I thought it would be better if I retired to this small, unfashionable hamlet and left Folkestone and London to you."

Sincerity dropped her gaze to her lap. Had she gone too far? Would her mother question her sincerity?

"It would have been better to come to me, Sincerity," said her father. Turning to his daughter's companion, he asked, "Did you know about Miss Granville's death before you left London, Miss Cobb?"

"No, my lord. But I know it was wrong of me to allow this pretense to continue. I will understand if you feel you must dismiss me."

"We will leave that matter for later. I'm sure this girl of mine is to blame. So, the question is, what are we to do now?"

"I do have a few questions for our daughter and for Miss Cobb, if you don't mind."

"Certainly not," Lord Hartford said, rising and moving toward the front windows where he could look out on the street.

"Where were you when that man was seducing my daughter, Miss Cobb?"

"I was not far away, my lady. They are practically betrothed, so I thought a few minutes alone would be acceptable."

"Obviously it was not for that odious barbarian."

"Mother, I will not have you speak about Simon in that manner."

"Simon, is it? The man is a Scot, for heaven's sake! He doesn't even wear breeches!"

"I think Simon looks quite attractive in his kilt. He has very good legs."

"Fetch my hartshorn and vinaigrette, Miss Cobb," wailed Lady Hartford.

"Never mind, Miss Cobb," said Lord Hartford, pouring his wife a glass of brandy. "Drink this, Divinity."

"Sincerity, I must agree with your mother on this. It looks very bad for this Simon fellow. I have made inquiries, and I know he is well able to afford a wife, even one as expensive as you are, but this whole business is too havey-cavey by half. It reflects very badly on him, courting a girl who is unprotected."

"I don't know why, Papa. We are unofficially betrothed. I mean, we only need your approval."

"And to announce it in the papers," said her father.

"No! That is, I don't want to announce it yet. We want to get to know each other better."

"It looked to me like you two know each other rather too well," observed her father dryly.

"But that was the first time we even kissed. Simon has been a perfect gentleman."

"I have only one other thing to ask, Sincerity, and I warn you, I have witnesses who can verify the truth of the matter. Has this Sir Simon been calling on you here?"

"Yes, Mother, but Miss Cobb was always nearby."

"That makes no difference. If he has been calling on you here, acting as if this were a brothel, then he has compromised you. Your father and I have discussed this at length. There is only one thing to do. While he is not the husband I would wish for a daughter of mine, I don't see any way to avoid it. You and Sir Simon McKendrick must wed as quickly as possible."

"No! I'll not have it!" shouted Sincerity, rising and shaking her fist at her mother.

"Sit down, Sincerity," commanded her father. Sincerity hesitated a moment, but she obeyed, her lips puckered in sullen defiance. "Your mother is right. I will pay a visit to Sir Simon this afternoon and demand that he wed you within the week."

"Papa, please . . ."

"I will brook no more arguments. Now, go to your room and stay there. If your betrothed has not been telling tales, he will call on you this evening with his proposal. Understood?"

"Yes, Papa, I understand. Cobbie, will you come with me?"

"No, we wish to speak to Miss Cobb alone," said her father.

Sincerity hung her head and left the room, heading for the back door and freedom instead of for the staircase.

"Miss Cobb, I know you have been with us for many years, serving us faithfully. But I'm afraid your handling of this incident has shaken our confidence in you," said Lord Hartford.

"You're right, my lord," whispered Cobbie, unable to face him. "I never should have allowed it to continue."

"I know you would not knowingly hurt Sincerity, but . . ."

A sneer on her face, Lady Hartford interrupted. "Lord Hartford is unaware of the extent of your scandalous behavior, Miss Cobb, but after speaking to Mr. Boynton at the assembly last night, I have the complete story! When I referred to this house as a brothel, I was not just speaking of my daughter's shocking behavior."

"Divinity! I must protest!"

"You're to pack your bags and be gone by tomorrow morning," said Lady Hartford, her expression as hard as nails.

"But . . ."

"Letitia, come here please," said Crispin, his nose out of joint and as high as Lady Hartford's. Miss Cobb moved swiftly to his side where he put a protective arm around her.

"How dare you speak to Miss Cobb in such a familiar manner," said Lady Hartford. "Perhaps you should look for a new position, too!"

"My name is Charles Crispin, my lady, since you seem to have forgotten it. And this is my wife, Mrs. Crispin."

"Your . . . wife?" exclaimed the Hartfords.

Lady Hartford slipped quietly to the floor. Lord Hartford

stepped over her and walked up to Miss Cobb. He leaned closer and gave her a peck on the cheek before extending his hand to the surprised butler.

"You had better take care of our Miss Cobb, Mr. Crispin. She's been more like a sister to me than an employee. There were times when I believe my wife and my daughters would have murdered each other were it not for her calming influence. So I say congratulations to you, Mr. Crispin, and best wishes to you, my dear Mrs. Crispin."

"Thank you, my lord. I will always remember your many kindnesses."

"So what shall we do with our little Sincerity?" he asked, looking back at his insensible spouse dispassionately.

"I think the first thing you should do, my lord, is speak to Sir Simon."

"Sir Simon, eh? So you are going to stick to that story of the betrothal? I would like to believe that Sincerity has found a husband, but I find it difficult to believe that a man of Sir Simon's maturity and temperment could have fallen head over heels in love with my scatterbrained daughter."

"Love is never what we expect, my lord," said Mrs. Crispin.

"And you are speaking from experience," he said, smiling slightly when the former governess nodded. "Very well. I will speak to the man. Do you have his direction?"

"The White Hart Inn, near the Pump Room, my lord," said Crispin.

"Thank you," he said, heading for the door. "Oh, and could you see about getting her up on the sofa? Thank you."

\* \* \*

"Simon, Simon, wake up!" hissed Sincerity, pulling at the counterpane, her eyes growing wide when she saw his bare chest.

"Ach! What do you think you're doin', girl? Get out of my bedroom!" he scolded, yanking the blanket out of her hands.

The spectacle of his chest hidden once again, Sincerity came to her senses and turned her back.

"I must speak to you immediately," she said.

"Sir Simon, did you call me? Oh, what th' blazes!" bellowed Angus when he stepped into his master's chamber.

"Angus, see to Miss Hartford—in the other room—while I dress. Sincerity, you are not to enter this room until I come out."

"Then hurry up, Simon. It is urgent!"

The desperation in her voice made him decide against dressing. Instead, he threw on a dressing gown, tied it securely, and entered the small sitting area where Sincerity sat on the edge of her chair, nervously biting her lower lip.

He dismissed his valet and joined her, sitting in the opposite chair, his knees touching hers.

"Just tell me everything, lass," he said softly.

Sincerity touched the bruise under his left eye, and he winced. "I'm so sorry, Simon. Sorry about that, sorry about everything."

"About everything?"

"Yes, everything has gone wrong. My father is going to demand that we wed. He says you compromised me. I know you didn't, but there is no reasoning with either of them!"

"So they plan to force you to wed me, and you don't want to," he said, hoping she would tell him he was wrong, hoping she would tell him she wanted nothing more than to marry him because she couldn't bear to live without him.

"Yes. I'm sorry. I never meant for this to happen."

"I know. You told me in the beginning that you didn't want to marry me or anybody." He rose and went to stand by the window. He saw Lord Hartford striding toward the inn and knew their time together was short. "What would you have me do, Sincerity?"

"You must refuse him, of course," she replied, but her voice had lost its resolve.

Simon turned and studied her in silence until the loud knocking began. Sincerity nearly jumped out of her skin.

"Hide," he commanded, and she dove under the writing desk.

Simon moved toward it, leaning against it casually before giving his visitor permission to enter.

"Sir Simon McKendrick, at your service, my lord," he said smoothly.

"How do you do?" responded Lord Hartford.

"I've been better," drawled Simon, touching his bruised face.

"I would apologize, but if you were a parent, you would understand why I felt compelled to plant you a facer. By the way, thank you for not retaliating."

Simon grinned for the first time. He turned to the decanters on the desk and offered his visitor a drink. Lord Hartford accepted and tossed off a glass of Madeira before clearing his throat, ready to get to the point.

"I've come here today to find out how you feel about my daughter."

"Oh?" asked Simon, surprised that Lord Hartford was being so civil. Perhaps Sincerity's story about being compromised was just that, another one of her stories.

"My wife thinks I am here to demand that you marry Sincerity."

"But you aren't?"

"I considered it, but I want Sincerity to be happy. I've never been able to make her mother happy, but I have tried to do better by my daughters."

"Then why have you come here?"

"I'm getting to that. You see, it occurred to me that you might just be a pawn in another of Sincerity's schemes, that you hadn't really been courting her, that you hadn't grown to care for her. You're obviously a man of the world. I made inquiries when Sincerity wrote to her mother about you. You weren't named, but my wife, with the help of an acquaintance here in Bath, a Lady Rutherford—perhaps you know her—was able to deduce who Sissie was talking about. She mentioned something about your drawings, and I had seen some of them in the *London Post,* some drawings of a boxing match. Quite good, by the way."

"I'm sure you didn't come here to talk about my drawings, my lord," said Sir Simon.

"No, I didn't. Anyway, I thought you probably don't care anything about my daughter, and you had no intention of marrying her. If that is the case, sir, I don't want to force you into marrying her, either."

"So you don't think I compromised her?"

"Shall we say, in the grander scheme of things, away from Bath, I think these little indiscretions will be overlooked."

"Then allow me to assure you, my lord, that Sincerity is everything I have ever wanted in a wife. I love her with all my heart, and I want to marry her as soon as possible."

"Are you absolutely certain, my boy?"

"I have never been more certain of anything in my entire life. If Sincerity will have me, I will marry her tomorrow. I don't know precisely how or when it happened, but I am madly in love with your daughter."

Simon's voice was soft and tender. It seemed he was

no longer speaking to her father, but to her. If she didn't know better, Sincerity would have believed him, too. She would give anything in the world if what he was saying were true. Tears glistened in her eyes. Simon was so noble, so brave to protect her after all she had done.

"Very well, my boy. Welcome to our family." Lord Hartford stepped forward and shook hands with Sir Simon. "Now all I have to do is go home and tell my wife that her new son-in-law is not a barbarian just because he is a Scotsman."

"Good luck, my lord. You might have better luck reminding her that I won't embarrass her by showing up for the Season in London. I can't stand the place."

"Now that just might work," laughed his lordship. "You'll join us for dinner tonight?"

"My pleasure. Until then," said Simon. Closing the door on his guest, he hurried across the room to help Sincerity rise.

"Sincerity, my sweet child," he said, squeezing her hands and holding her at arm's length. "Do you think that will smooth things over for you?"

Sincerity threw her arms around his neck with wild abandon. She found it impossible to resist the pleasure of one last embrace. She could not, of course, allow him to martyr himself by marrying her, but the thought of never seeing his handsome face again filled her heart with despair.

Hiding her face in the heavy silk brocade of his dressing gown, she wanted to pretend . . . But no, not this time. Simon's vows of love were for her father's benefit, not hers. It was all part of their carefully planned act. It would be unscrupulous of her to hold him to his words, and for once in her life, she vowed to be true and honorable. Simon deserved nothing less.

If only time would stand still, letting this magic moment last forever, she thought, clinging to him as if her life depended on it. If only he would lift her chin and kiss her, tell her to her face that he loved her and wanted her to be his wife.

"You should go," Simon announced finally, stepping away from her and tugging at his dressing gown to make certain he was still decent.

"Should I?" she managed to say, stealing one last look at his dear countenance.

He kissed her forehead like a big brother might and turned her toward the door. "Yes, you should leave now before I forget I am a gentleman. I'll see you tonight," he added, resisting the urge to give her backside a gentle pat to send her on her way.

Sincerity hired a chair to return to Russell Street. She wasn't certain how she managed it, but she arrived before her father and hurried to the drawing room where her mother still lay on the sofa, a cup of lukewarm coffee laced with brandy at her elbow.

Taking a deep breath, gathering her resolve around her, she said calmly, "Mother, we must talk."

"I don't think I am up to any more conversation with you today, Sincerity," replied her mother feebly. "The world has gone mad."

"Then you need only listen," said Sincerity, who proceeded to confess to everything, allowing the truth to flow like water.

"So you never planned to wed this Sir Simon, this Scotsman?" demanded her mother.

"Never."

"Thank goodness for that!" said Divinity Hartford, sitting up and smiling at her daughter for the first time.

"Yes, I thought you would be pleased," murmured Sincerity, her melancholy overtaking her for a moment. "So can we please just go home to Folkestone, Mother?"

"What about Bath? I thought you wanted to stay here." Her mother could never resist taunting her.

"No, I just want to go home. The sooner, the better."

"Very well. Then go upstairs and start packing. Perhaps Miss Cobb—I mean, Mrs. Crispin—will help you."

"So you know about Miss Cobb?"

"Yes, but I refuse to discuss it. Pack your things. We will leave first thing in the morning."

"Thank you, Mother."

Sincerity climbed the stairs with a heavy tread, her spirits low. Cobbie and Trudy were nowhere to be found, so she asked her mother's abigail to help her. Marnie, who had wrangled her way to the position of Lady Hartford's personal dresser by telling tales on Sincerity and her sisters, was only too happy to help.

Downstairs, Lord Hartford entered the drawing room, fresh from his gratifying conversation with Sir Simon, and ready to make his daughter happy beyond her wildest hopes.

"She's upstairs packing," was his wife's brief response when he asked where Sincerity was.

"Packing? Why is she packing?"

Lady Hartford explained Sincerity's story in every damning detail, ending with a pleased little laugh.

"I don't think she will ever tell a lie again," she concluded smugly.

"We'll see about that," he declared, climbing the stairs to speak to his daughter firsthand.

"Sincerity, your mother tells me you don't want to marry Sir Simon after all. Is that right?"

"Yes, Papa. I never intend to marry."

"What if he wants to wed you?"

"I'm sure he does not," she replied concisely, her reticence speaking volumes to her loving father.

"Very well. If that is what you wish," he said, kissing her cheek and leaving her alone again.

The tears she had been holding back began to flow in

earnest, and Sincerity had to discontinue her task until she could control her emotions again.

Lord Hartford hurried back to the White Hart Inn, hoping to catch Sir Simon before he went out. His luck was in. Simon was just finishing his bath when Angus informed him of his lordship's return.

"What the deuce does he want now?" he muttered, climbing out of the warm water and toweling off quickly. Once again, he threw on his dressing gown.

"Hello again," he said.

"No time for the niceties. I came to tell you that my daughter has convinced her mother that all she wants to do is go home to Folkestone."

"What? When did this happen?"

"In the past hour. I took my time getting home, but by the time I arrived, Sincerity was half packed. I just thought you should know. You won me over, Sir Simon. If you were serious, you had best hurry to Russell Street and convince my daughter."

Without bothering to say his farewells, Simon turned on his heel and stalked back into his bedchamber. Grabbing a shirt and his kilt, he threw them on, shoving his feet into his dancing shoes since they were the closest at hand.

How dare she! How dare she gull him into falling in love with her and then turn her back on him! And there she was, just a snip of a girl! Not only that, but she had accepted his embraces, she had listened to his vow of love, and now she was running away! Well, he would just see about that!

Striding through the streets, his hair blowing in the wind, he looked the picture of a barbaric Scotsman. When he threw open the front door, Crispin blocked his path.

"Out of the way, Crispin. I'm in no mood for heroics."

The butler grinned and stepped aside.

Lady Hartford materialized at the foot of the stairs.

"I want to speak to your daughter," he said.

"Never! She doesn't want to see you!"

"Sincerity!" he roared. "Where the devil are you?"

"Sir Simon!" screamed Lady Hartford as he brushed her aside.

"Sincerity!" he roared again, this time picking Lady Hartford up and thrusting her at the butler.

Taking the steps two at a time, he thundered, "Sincerity! I want to talk to you!"

He threw open the door to Miss Cobb's bedroom, then the sitting-room door, and finally discovered Sincerity's room. Her mother's maid dropped the gown she was holding, her eyes wide with fright.

"Get out!" he barked, and she scurried away.

"Sir Simon!" came Lady Hartford's outraged cry again as she clawed at his shirtsleeve.

Simon picked her up one more time, shoved her into the room across the hall, and turned the key. With an angry grunt, he sent the maid scurrying down the hall.

Entering Sincerity's room again, he slammed the door and locked it. Striding across to the sitting-room door, he closed it, too, turning the key before whirling to face his beloved.

Hah! he thought. Arms folded, legs braced, and a scowl of pure rage marring his handsome face, he demanded, "What the devil are you about, leaving Bath without so much as a by-your-leave?"

Sincerity Hartford had changed since her arrival in Bath. The taste of independence had emboldened her, and the past twenty-four hours had tempered her like fine steel. Now she faced him without flinching, her blue eyes snapping with icy brilliance. "I might ask the same of you, Simon, coming into my house, into my room, turning out my abigail and my mother without so much as a by-your-leave," she said, throwing his words back at him. "And to speak to me in such a manner! I'll not have it, Simon McKendrick! Now, if you have something to say to me, then pray get on with it. I have packing to do!"

Sincerity braced for his outburst, but Simon only took a turn around the room once before sitting down on the side of the bed. She swallowed hard, her eyes wide with doubt and the tiniest glimmer of hope.

His bronzed face creased with an appreciative smile, Simon looked up at her and said softly, "I must tell you, lass, I've not been so handily put in my place since my wife passed away. Come here t' me." When Sincerity didn't move, he added, "Please."

She moved to stand in front of him, and he patted the bed. She hesitated and then sat down, allowing him to take her hand in his.

"When I married my Annie, I was a mere lad. Two years later, she died in childbirth, along with the babe."

"I'm so sorry, Simon," Sincerity whispered tearfully.

"Afterward, I left Scotland to fight Napoleon. But we finished with him, and I found myself back home, not quite knowing what to do with myself."

He turned to face her while his fingers carressed her hand. "After Annie, I never planned to wed again, never wanted to. And then I met you. The first time I took you in my arms, I knew what I'd been missing and why I had become so restless. I knew I wanted you."

"Simon, I . . ."

He placed a gentle finger on her lips and shook his head. Letting his hand fall, he continued. "This morning, when I was talking to your father, my heart was speaking to you. Couldn't you hear, lass? I want to marry you, not as a favor to you or any other creature on this earth, but for the most selfish reason in the world, for me, for my soul. You complete me."

He lifted her hand and kissed her palm. With a flicker of a smile, he added, "And there I was, not even realizing my life was incomplete. Say you'll marry me, Sincerity. Say you love me."

"I do, Simon. I love you with all my heart!"

"And you won't run away?" he asked, lifting her chin so he could look deep into her eyes Sincerity shook her head. "Promise?" She nodded. "Then kiss me, lass, until your mother manages to break down that door!"

Sincerity fell into his arms. Their lips met with hungry abandon, and they collapsed onto the bed, shutting out the distant knocking and Lady Hartford's shrill command to "Open up!"

---

Donna Bell welcomes comments from her readers and can be contacted at Kensington Publishing or by e-mail at dondonbell@netscape.net

---